NEEDLED

A Quilters Club Mystery

NEEDLED

A Quilters Club Mystery

Marjory Sorrell Rockwell

ABSOLUTELY AMAZING eBOOKS

ABSOLUTELY AMAZING eBOOKS

Published by Whiz Bang LLC, 926 Truman Avenue, Key West, Florida 33040, USA.

For information contact:
Publisher@AbsolutelyAmazingEbooks.com

ISBN-13: 978-1945772313 (Absolutely Amazing Ebooks)
ISBN-10: 194577231X

"When one has tasted watermelon, he knows what the angels eat."

- Mark Twain

Other Quilters Club Mysteries
By Marjory Sorrell Rockwell

The Quilters Club Quartet

The Underhanded Stitch

The Patchwork Puzzler

Coming Unraveled

Hemmed In

Sewed Up Tight

All Tangled Up

A Christmas Quilt: The Prequel

Available from
AbsolutelyAmazingEbooks.com

NEEDLED

A Quilters Club Mystery

CHAPTER ONE

The Stroke

Maddy Madison had been in the hospital for barely a week, but that was enough time for someone to murder her doctor. Dr. Kardashian had died in the hospital's parking lot, dropped dead just as he was stepping into his shiny new Mercedes Benz AMG S63. The toxicology report showed traces of a substance known as polonium. You can't get polonium poisoning by shaking hands or touching a doorknob. A closer inspection revealed a tiny pinprick on the soft underside of Dr. Kardashian's forearm.

That's a fine how-do-you-do, thought Maddy. *Now I'll have to find myself a new doctor.*

Dr. Elmer Kardashian was considered the best vascular neurologist this side of Indianapolis. Fortunately for Maddy, another stroke doctor was waiting in the wings, an associate of Dr. K's who had offices in the same medical center. J. Hewitt Blatt, MD, PhD, and BMBS normally took over Dr. K's patients when the old duffer went on vacation, so the switchover was quite seamless. Well, for everyone except Dr. K.

~ ~ ~

Maddy wasn't about to let a little thing like a stroke keep her down. She took to physical therapy like a Jane Fonda workout tape played at fast forward. Yes, being in her late fifties, Maddy remembered Jane Fonda ... and Betamax VCRs.

Maddy's husband – Beauregard Hollingsworth Madison IV, or Beau for short – was a Vietnam vet and still referred to the movie star (cum workout guru) as "Hanoi Jane." He carried a grudge. Likely always would.

Maddy didn't remember much about her stroke. One minute she was helping the Quilters Club solve crimes; the next she was in the Burpyville hospital. "Bummer," she said to Beau. He knew she didn't like missing her weekly quilting bees.

The Quilters Club was a group of four women – five if you counted Maddy's thirteen-year-old granddaughter – who enjoyed making patchwork quilts.

They were like fingers on the hand of friendship: Bootsie Purdue, wife of the town's police chief; Cookie Bentley, head of the local Historical Society, married to a successful farmer; Lizzie Ridenour, whose spouse was a retired bank president; and, of course, Madelyn Agnes Madison, whose hubby was a former mayor of Caruthers Corners, the small town in Indiana where they had lived all their lives.

Named after her Grammy, Agnes Tidemore – her friends called her Aggie – was kind of like an apprentice, still learning the intricacies of quiltmaking. The group mainly did patchwork or pieced quilts: Half Square Triangles, Tumblers, Strips, you name it. Motifs ranged from Farmer's Wife to Jelly Roll Race 1600, Honeycomb, Bears Paw, Wedding Ring, Lone Star, and Jacob's Ladder – as well as Postage Stamp Quilts, Cathedral Window Quilts, Charm Quilts, and Crazy Quilts. But the gals had been known to venture as far afield as Appliqué Quilts, Art Quilts, and Paper Piercing.

Truth was, Aggie liked making quilts ... but better still she loved unraveling mysteries. The Quilters Club had tackled its fair share of local crimes. Aggie thought of it as an unofficial detective agency.

Being semi-bedridden didn't stop Maddy from sniffing out mysteries. She was determined to look into Dr. Kardashian's death. After all, here she lay in her sterile white hospital room, with nothing to do but think about the good doctor's murder.

Her visitors brought her clues instead of flowers.

CHAPTER TWO

Brain Attack

Every year, more than 800,000 people in the United States have a stroke. 1 in 6 people will experience one in their lifetime. Strokes remain the #1 cause of disability in adults.

There are two types of strokes: hemorrhagic or ischemic. Maddy had suffered the ischemic variety. That's when a vessel supplying blood to the brain becomes blocked. The FDA-approved treatment for ischemic strokes is the intravenous administration of a recombinant tissue plasminogen activator (tPA). The tPA dissolves the clot and improves blood flow to the brain.

This must be given within 4.5 hours after the symptoms of a stroke.

A stroke cuts off the blood supply to brain tissue. Every minute a stroke goes untreated two million brain cells die. That's 14-billion synapses and 7.5 miles of myelinated fibers gone every minute. It is critical that a stroke be treated as soon as possible.

Shortly after Maddy's son Freddie became the Caruthers Corners fire chief, he'd added a paramedic unit. His crack response team delivered Maddy at the emergency room within fifteen minutes. They fed her aspirin all the way.

Fortunately, Burpyville Memorial was certified as a Primary Stroke Center, meaning it had vascular neurologists on staff, ready to spring into action. Their motto was "Time is Brain."

For the past three days Maddy had been visited in her room by a never-ending parade of neurologists, phlebotomists, physiatrists, radiologists, dieticians, nurses aids, and physical therapists. Even medical students came by to stare at her as if she were a lab rat.

Luckily for Maddy, there was no discernable damage to the brain. Perhaps a small loss of memory for the hours leading up to the event, but that seemed to be all. Well, all she could remember not remembering.

Technically, Maddy had suffered a TIA (Transient Ischemic Attack), which is defined as a temporary stroke that causes no lasting damage. Whew!

The good news: The central nervous system is adaptive and can recover most of its functions. To some degree the brain can heal itself through a process called neuroplasticity. Stroke rehabilitation commonly starts within 24 to 48 hours, during the patient's acute hospital stay.

~ ~ ~

"You've got to break me out of here," pleaded Maddy, but her friend Bootsie Purdue was having none of it. As wife of the Caruthers Corners police chief, she wasn't about to sanction any skips.

"Relax," said Cookie Bentley. "You could use a little time off."

"I've got fings to do," she insisted. Still a slight slur to her speech, but that was clearing up.

"Like what?" said Lizzie Ridenour, brushing wisps of her red hair off her face. "I know I'd enjoy laying around in bed, watching television, and eating bonbons." Everybody knew Lizzie was hooked on TV soap operas.

"I don't think bonbons are on my approved diet plan," sighed Maddy. She'd spent a session that morning with a dietician, who insisted she loose 20 pounds and give up fried foods. But how would any self-respecting Hoosier live without fried pork tenderloins?

~ ~ ~

The dietician had been firm. "Healthy food habits can reduce the three risk factors for stroke — poor cholesterol levels, high blood pressure and excess weight. Diets high in saturated fat and trans fat can raise blood cholesterol levels. Diets high in sodium can contribute to increased blood pressure. And high-calorie diets can contribute to obesity. All increase the stroke risk."

At 140 pounds, Maddy supposed she could afford to shed a little weight. But she was a lightweight compared to Bootsie. The pudgy brunette had tipped the scales at 180 since college. Cookie was the most normal, a former beauty queen who ate sensibly. Lizzie was on the skinny side. As Beau said, "She could use a few cheeseburgers."

The dietician advised, "Five or more servings of fruits and vegetables a day can reduce the risk of stroke. Try it."

"That cow's already out of the barn," snorted Maddy. "Why do you think I'm here in this hospital bed?"

"You don't want any return visits, do you? Recurrences account for one out of every four strokes."

"That's scary."

"Doesn't have to be, you eat right."

Maddy sighed. There goes all those watermelon cookies and upside down watermelon cakes. Fat pills with the amount of sugar she put in them. Paula Deen had nothing on her. She usually bought confectionary sugar in 50 lb. bags.

Beau would be unhappy if the steady supply of cookies and cakes and pies dried up. His metabolism allowed him to eat like a horse, yet not gain an ounce. Beau Madison was well over 6 foot, a James Cromwell type. A beanpole, if you wanted to describe him. He had excelled in basketball back in high school. Flash, they had called him. But that had been over thirty years ago. He moved a little slower these days.

So did Maddy. At least before the stroke. She wasn't moving at all now, not unless she had a physical therapist beside her as she did the treadmill on slow while holding tightly to the handlebars.

~ ~ ~

"So what's the scoop?" coaxed Maddy. She knew the night nurse's sister, so they had developed a sort of temporary friendship.

Natalie Thackeray was busy adjusting the thermostat. Maddy had complained that the room was too cold. "Scoop on what? Your prognosis? What the doctors aren't telling you? Do all those pills on your night table really work? What scoop are you looking for?"

"How did Dr. Kardashian really die? I bet you've seen the coroner's report."

"Sure I have. But that's confidential till the coroner chooses to release it."

Maddy smiled winningly. "So what's the big deal if you tell me a few hours ahead of his press conference?"

"Cause of death is still officially unknown. But it certainly wasn't natural, you can trust me on that."

"Murder, you're saying?"

"Nobody has used that word yet," said Nurse Thackeray. "But I'd say it's a sure bet."

~ ~ ~

"Did jew take over all uff Dr. Kardashian's patients?" asked Maddy. Speaking was still a little difficult.

Dr. Blatt looked up from his clipboard. "Yes, his death was rather sudden, so we didn't have a chance to divide them up between doctors. My caseload doubled overnight."

"Do you haf the same schedule azz he did?"

He nodded. "Pretty much."

"May I see," she indicated his clipboard.

He shrugged. "Sure, why not?"

As she looked over his schedule, she flipped the pages back to the day Dr. Kardashian died. She didn't have the near-photographic memory of her friend Cookie, but she tried to memorize the names and order of the people Dr. K had seen prior to collapsing in the parking lot.

"Here, give it back," Dr. Blatt said, reaching for his clipboard. "I've got rounds to make."

~ ~ ~

Aggie walked home from school as usual. She liked to linger around the bandstand in the town square. Sometimes high school boys were there playing their guitars. She would be going to Caruthers High next year. Boys didn't interest her yet, at least not in a romantic way. But she liked to listen to their music.

She could see her home from here, the big blue Victorian known as "the Taylor house," looming there, straight across the square. Her Grammy had grown up in that house, her maiden name being Taylor. She was worried about her grandmother, still in the hospital. But her Mom said she was making an amazing recovery, would be almost as good as new.

Nevertheless, she doubted if her Grammy would finish the quilt she'd been sewing in time for Watermelon Days. Too bad, it had been shaping up to be one of her best – a Log Cabin Courthouse Steps pattern, using wool challis fabrics. A feast of rich colors, the quilt was accented with a 5-inch wide paisley border, red silk ribbon ties at the four corners of each block, and an applied brown silk grosgrain ribbon for the binding.

Aggie had been working on a Crazy Quilt, one of those hodgepodge patchworks with a scrap of every fabric in the bin – silks, velvets, chenille, and threads of every hue. Wool challis binding, reverse tied, flannel backing. But she didn't expect to win a prize. Her sewing was still too sloppy, although Lizzie was making good progress in teaching her how to do embroidery stitches – the chain stitch, chevron stitch, French knot, feather stitch, even the crisscrossed cretan stitch.

From where Aggie sat on the steps of the bandstand, almost in the shadow of the four bronze statues honoring the Hoople Quadruplets, a hometown foursome, she could see the brick façade of the Town Hall where her father worked. That building and this grassy square were the heart of Caruthers Corners. It was said the early settlers circled their wagons here to protect themselves from marauding Potawatomi Indians.

As she watched the Town Hall, she saw a stretch limousine pull up in front of the building. A sleek black vehicle, it reminded her of a dachshund, those elongated examples of the canine world. Well, this was an elongated version of a Cadillac, the proportions exaggerated. She recognized the passenger who stepped out of the limo and entered the brick building: It was Hitch Richardson, the movie star. She'd seen a rerun of his recent movie – *The Riders of the Lost Ark II* – on TV the other night. What was a famous Hollywood star doing in a tiny Midwestern town like Caruthers Corners?

CHAPTER THREE

On the Case

Maddy talked an orderly into giving her an outing in a wheelchair. "I'd like to get a little fresh air," she told him convincingly.

Joe Turner was a large man with jailhouse tattoos nearly invisible against his dark skin. His hair was cropped close, tight curls outlining his male pattern baldness. He wore blue scrubs. "Where you wanna go?" he asked, heading the wheelchair down the hallway with little regard for the safety of patients and nurses in its path.

"I want to visit my friend Mrs. Gilbert in Room 337," she instructed.

Turned out Mrs. Gilbert had died during the night. Nothing suspicious in that, being she was 97.

"Now let's check on Mrs. Aebischer in Room 352," Maddy changed their course.

"You don't seem too broken up over losing your friend," Joe Turner observed.

"Mrs. Gilbert enjoyed a long and productive life," she said with a wave of her hand. "Onward to Room 352."

Cordelia Aebischer was a blue-haired lady in her 80s. She was happy to have the company. "Yes, Dr. Kardashian saw me around 9 a.m. on the day he died," she recounted. "He seemed under the weather. Stood well back from my bed. Said he might be coming down with a cold."

Eunice Keller, who Dr. K called on at 10 a.m., had a

similar story. So did Mr. Schmid, who he saw at 11:15. Ernie Schmid recalled that Dr. K had used his bathroom, throwing up, based on the retching sounds. Mrs. Meier in 210 said he canceled his 12:15 appointment with her, the nurse saying he was going home early. By 12:27 he was dead in the parking lot, having just opened the door of his Mercedes Benz before collapsing.

No need to talk with other patients on the list, not that she remembered them all anyway. Facts were clear, Dr. K was already sick the morning he died.

~ ~ ~

Maddy dispatched her friend Lizzie to pay a sympathy call on Dr. K's wife, Veronica. She was an elegant blonde wearing more gold jewelry than a drug dealer. Her eyes were red from crying.

The flowers Lizzie brought with her were lovely, a pink arrangement of roses, larkspur, carnations, and Asiatic lilies in a white basket. She had picked them up at Personally Yours Flowers & Gifts, the shop owned by Cookie's brother-in-law..

While Veronica Kardashian had never met the wife of the former president of Caruthers Corners Savings and Loan, she assumed this was just another of Elmer's many patients and accepted the flowers as a sign of respect for her late husband.

"Yes, he was feeling punky the night before he ... passed," Veronica said. "I remember he came home that evening complaining of a headache."

~ ~ ~

Bootsie had an assignment of her own. She drove out to the Burpyville Vista Golf Club and spoke with the pro. A private club with an 18-hole course designed by the great Sean Bascom, the wide green fairways offered three Par-4s. *Golf Digest* called it "imminently playable."

"Yeah, I remember Elmer playing a round the day before he popped off. When I saw him he was pretty chipper, feeling at the top of his game. As I recall he made a hole-in-one on the fourth hole."

The Club's bartender remembered Elmer having a round of drinks with his golf partners before leaving for home. A gin and tonic as usual. "Asked for an extra glass of ice. Must've been a hard game. He was complaining about being overheated. He face was all sweaty."

Also Bootsie stopped off to see Big Jack Tatum, owner of Tatum's Pontiac. The golf pro had identified Big Jack as being one of Dr. K's foursome. She found him at the dealership, going over ad copy for the next day's *Burpyville Gazette*. He was a handsome guy with curly blonde hair, a Preppy type. His outfit was straight out of J. Crew. He was what people described as a "gladhander." You often saw him on TV hawking his cars: "*Once you buy from Big Jack, you're sure to come back!*"

"Elmer started feeling bad around the sixteenth hole," Big Jack pinpointed it. "Said his stomach was upset. He thought it might have been the fish he had for lunch. Baked flounder was the special that day. We all had it, but he was the only one feeling sickly."

Her route home passed right by Burpyville Memorial, so Bootsie stopped off and gave her report to Maddy in person. It was easier that way when everything was fresh in her mind.

CHAPTER FOUR

The Movie Star

"**D**ad, what was Handsome Hitch doing at the Town Hall today?"

"Who?"

"Hitch Richardson, the movie star. I saw him pull up in a big limo."

"Oh, you mean Richard Hitchinson. That was his name before he became an actor. He was my college roommate. He's thinking of building a getaway home here in Caruthers Corners."

"You know Hitch Richardson?"

"Sure, I know Richie. We shared a room at Harvard. I've seen him in his underwear," her father teased.

"Me too," said Tilly. She used to visit Mark in Boston while he was in school. They were dating by then. Her parents hadn't approved of those long weekends away from home, but Tilly was known to be headstrong, just like her mother. Tilly and Mark had married right after his graduation from law school.

"You've seen Hitch Richardson in his underwear?" exclaimed Aggie. Her world taking a new spin.

"He was just Richie back then. Always running around the apartment in his tighty-whities. Quite the clown." Tilly was amused at her daughter's fascination with this movie star A-Lister.

"And you guys never told me you knew Handsome

Hitch?" That's what *People Magazine* had dubbed him when recently picking him as "Sexiest Man Alive."

Her father chuckled. "Richie is just Richie. He's a better big-screen action hero than he was a tax lawyer."

"Yes," Tilly continued the story, "Richie got recruited to the same law firm as your father in Los Angeles. He was about to get fired when a talent scout discovered him walking down Hollywood Boulevard, looking at those stars in the sidewalk. Suddenly he was making straight-to-video movies, sort of a Poor Man's Harrison Ford. His big break came when he scored a small speaking role in one of the *Star Wars* blockbusters. That's when his career took off."

"I loved him in *The Riders of the Lost Ark II*," gushed Aggie, obviously star struck. "I almost peed in my panties when he saved the princess from that three-headed monster."

"That rip-off wasn't one of his better films," laughed her father. "His latest picture – *Sunset and Moonrise* – is getting Oscar buzz. Or so he tells me."

"And he's moving to Caruthers Corners?"

"That remains to be seen. Richie bought some land out on Far Fields Road, but he's having trouble with the title. Seems it used to be an old weather station, part of the National Weather Service's Automated Surface Observing System. It was closed down over thirty years ago, but recently the government sold it off at auction. Richie bought the land, with the idea of building a getaway home there."

"Talk about a perfect place for a getaway home," said Tilly. "Nobody ever goes out to Far Fields Road except maybe romantic teenagers."

~ ~ ~

Beau Madison found himself at a complete loss with Maddy in the hospital. Their daughter Tilly came over every day, her three children in tow, to fix his dinners.

For breakfast he made do with cereal – Honey Nut Cheerios. This was the most popular cereal in America. It used to contain real nuts, but in 2006 that had been replaced by flavorings to simulate the nut taste. Now General Mills uses peach and apricot pits to create the "natural almond flavor." Oh well.

Most days he took his lunch at the Cozy Café on Main Street, usually meeting Bootsie's husband Jim for that midday repast. Jim Purdue was not only his best friend since high school, he was the town's police chief. Beau liked to joke that he'd known Jim since he'd had wavy hair. Jim Purdue's hairline had been receding even in the 12th grade.

The two men were physical opposites: Jim Purdue was stocky and bald as Beau was lanky and bushy headed. Jim hadn't set foot in Mo's Barber Shop in years; Beau was usually overdue for a haircut.

Today, they were having their usual. Beau munching on a fried pork tenderloin while Jim partook of the Cozy Special: Hot Dog with Pork and Beans. Nobody was sure why it was called a Special, since that particular delicacy was listed on the lunch menu at least four times a week. Van Camp's Pork and Beans was very popular around here, the recipe for beans in tomato sauce created in 1889 by the son of an Indianapolis grocer.

Maisie came over to refill their coffee. "How's Maddy?" the waitress asked as she poured the freshly brewed Maxwell House into their cups. Cozy Café was known for its coffee ... and watermelon pie.

"She's mending," replied Beau. As a descendent of a town founder – not to mention being a former mayor – everybody hereabouts knew the Madisons. Forget NSA's spy program, there were no secrets in a small town like Caruthers Corners.

"Tell her folks are missing her."

"You bet." Beau thought it ironic, his wife had been in the hospital only four days and people were reacting as if she had disappeared from the face of the earth. Maddy usually spent a longer time in Chicago when visiting their son Bill and his wife Amanda.

Bill and Amanda had been having a spot of trouble lately, but they had put aside their differences to drive down to visit Maddy in the hospital. Their adopted son N'yen came along, happy to miss a couple days of summer camp. The boy and Tilly's daughter Aggie were "best-est of friends." Their equivalent of BFFs.

"Well, give her our hello," said the waitress, sidling back toward the stainless-steel counter. Maisie Walters had been slinging hash at Cozy Café since high school. She'd been in the same class as Beau and Maddy and all their friends. Maisie hadn't been part of the "in" group, but everybody liked her.

Beau turned back to his luncheon partner. "Anything new on Dr. K?" he asked, just to be making conversation. "Rumor has it that his death wasn't from natural causes." He'd been talking with Maddy.

"Just what my counterpart down in Burpyville tells me: 'Mysterious Circumstances' is the exact term he used. Glad it's not my case."

"Do you think he OD'ed on something? I hear how

doctors sometimes get hooked on their own drugs, being able to write prescriptions for themselves."

"Who knows? Drugs aren't that hard to come by without a script these days. Frank busted a meth lab last week."

Frank Crenshaw was police chief over in Burpyville, but he'd gone to Caruthers High with Jim and Beau. They had all been on the football team. But that was a dim memory from back in the early '70s.

~ ~ ~

Cookie's husband Ben Bentley had twice won the state wrestling championship in high school. Now a successful farmer, the burly man was Cookie's second husband, her first having died in a tragic tractor accident (nobody should ever wear a necktie while plowing).

These days Ben spent most of his time helping administer the Haney Bros. Zoo and Exotic Animal Refuge, the town's main tourist attraction. He'd donated the land for it. Considering himself semi-retired from agricultural pursuits, he leased out his remaining fields to soybean growers. Back in the day, he'd grown watermelons on them.

At one time watermelons were the county's main crop, prompting its annual Watermelon Days every summer. The festival would be coming up in a couple of weeks. Everybody was excited.

CHAPTER FIVE

Watermelons

The first recorded evidence of a watermelon crop occurred over 5,000 years ago in Egypt. Hieroglyphics show that watermelons were placed in the tombs of pharaohs. Today, varieties of the warm-season melons range from 1-pound icebox varieties to 100-pound contest entries. Carolina Cross melons, the most common kind grown around here, average about 50 pounds.

The watermelon (*Citrullus vulgaris*) is actually a member of the gourd family, with smooth green skin, red pulp, and watery juice.

As singer Enrico Caruso once said, "Watermelon – it's a good fruit. You eat, you drink, you wash your face."

Harvested between July and Labor Day, the watermelon is the most consumed melon in the United States. Over 6 percent of all watermelons grown in the US come from Indiana. Each harvesting season, more than 7,500 acres of watermelons are grown in Indiana and Illinois – the areas overseen by the Illiana Watermelon Association.

Watermelons reach harvest in 65 to 90 days. Smaller varieties are usually ready before larger ones. Watermelons that run 2 to 4 pounds include Early Midget, Garden Baby, Golden Midget, Little Baby Flower, Sugar Baby, and Petite Sweet. Larger melons like Black Diamond, Navajo Sweet, King and Queen, Charleston Gray, and Moon and Stars require 90 days or more to ripen.

Watermelon Days is a weeklong celebration of this favorite crop during the late summer. The date is chosen by lottery each year. Main Street gets closed off from the Town Hall down to Moe's Barbershop, lined with tented stalls that sell baked goods, handicrafts, shaved ice, wood whittlings, knitted caps, paintings, quilted goods, fried cheese balls, jewelry, wind chimes, hot dogs, and sand candles. In the town square Hoagie Henderson & His Hoosier All-Stars play in the canopied bandstand, while families picnic on the grass, couples stroll, and squealing children wade in the knee-deep pond next to the bronze statue honoring Beau Madison's great-great-grandfather. There are poetry recitations, a quiltmaking competition, and the traditional watermelon-eating contest.

Keith Blickensderfer's brother-in-law – Fat Karl Schaeffer – had won the watermelon-eating contest the past two years in a row. No one was surprised because Fat Karl was kinda shaped like a watermelon. He was married to Keith's sister Wanda. One of Keith's boys was named after him.

Watermelon Days always started off with an invocation by one of the local ministers, this year it being the turn of Rev. Durrenberger, pastor of First Mennonite Church. That would be followed by a short speech from the town's mayor, that being Aggie's dad, Mark Tidemore. Then, as head of the Caruthers Corner Historical Society, Cookie Bentley would give a brief overview of the town's one-time reputation as "the Watermelon Capital of Indiana."

In recent years, the festival has featured a parade down Main Street, like a conga line edging past the lineup of stalls.

The parade is usually comprised of the town's only fire engine, a Boy Scout troop, the high school band, and assorted animals from Haney Bros. Zoo and Exotic Animal Refuge. Happy the elephant is always a favorite. Amid all this, a stampede of colorful clowns race up and down the street, weaving between the paraders and into the crowds, scaring little kids and hugging their mothers.

For most of a week Watermelon Days presented 4H displays, a calf judging contest, pig wrestling, a science fair, and its highlight: the Biggest Watermelon competition, an event open to all local farmers.

Ben Bentley had won it one year, but lately Boyd Aitkens had been coming in with first place. Last year's winning melon weighed in at 312 pounds. The Guinness World Records lists the World's Heaviest Watermelon as 350.5 pounds, grown by Chris Kent of Sevierville, Tennessee, so ol' Boyd had made a credible showing.

The festival ends with the crowning of the Watermelon Days Queen. Odds-on favorite this year was Missy Yager's daughter, Cindy, at 18 a blonde goddess in the sweet spot of young womanhood. Missy was a former Queen herself (1998).

Maddy was getting anxious that her quilt wasn't completed. But it was close. She wondered if she could hold a needle well enough to finish it off.

She asked her daughter Tilly to bring the quilt and her sewing paraphernalia to the hospital. It would give her something to do, sitting there in the bed like an ... well, like an invalid. She'd never considered how boring an imposed stay in a hospital could be.

CHAPTER SIX

The Plumber

Harry "Hopalong Cassidy" Casals was a retired pipefitter from Chicago. He'd lived in Caruthers Corners since the mid-'70s when he came down here on a government contract. After completing his work on the project, he decided to stick around. That's when he started Hoppy's Plumbing & Refrigeration, a small one-man shop located on Fourth Avenue near the US Post Office.

Hoppy's Plumbing had provided him with a decent living. But it hadn't delivered the life of luxury he'd dreamed of since growing up in the South Side projects. Chicago is divided into three sections, the North Side and the West Side being the other two. There is no East Side due to the location of Lake Michigan. Residents of the South Side reflect a great disparity in income. And Hoppy's family was among the have-nots.

Tough toogies. He'd remedied his lifestyle considerably when he appreticed with a large industrial pipefitting concern. And it got better when he became a Journeyman. He climbed one more rung up the income ladder when he took that contract with the US Air Force.

Recently he'd sold his plumbing business and retired, taking his max Social Security dole. But finances were tight. That's why he listened to the proposition a man made to him in a Burpyville bar. $50,000 for a little "plumbing" job. Not bad for a night's work.

~ ~ ~

Maddy's granddaughter Aggie had gone over to Caruthers Corners Historical Society with Bootsie and Lizzie. As executive secretary for the non-profit organization, Cookie wanted to show off the new wing built by a donation from the Hoople Quadruplets Trust Fund.

The town's most famous figures, the Hoople Quadruplets – Herbert, Hilda, Helga, and Helena – had put Caruthers Corners on the map when a feature about the multiple births appeared in *Life* Magazine. However, they were all gone now, except for Hilda. She still lived in the big mansion atop Hoople Hill, all her bills paid for by the Trust. These days she devoted herself to worthy causes, like building that new wing for the Historical Society.

"Wow, this is TD," said Aggie as she took in the new facility. Slang for "amazing."

The new exhibit space was indeed to die for. About the size of a basketball court, it featured a high slanted ceiling with four large skylights. Glass cases lined the fabric-covered walls, displaying various historical artifacts – a stovepipe hat said to have been worn by Lincoln, assorted Indian arrowheads, invertebrate fossils, a collection of old bottles, small stuffed animals (otter, badger, cottontail, etc.), several family Bibles displaying genealogy charts, even a bowling-ball-sized meteorite that had landed near here back in 1968. On the far wall, under perfect lighting, hung the Society's rare Renaissance Quilt; the centerpiece of the room. In the middle of the floor was a large Conestoga, a replica of the covered wagon that broke down here in 1829, leading to the founding of Caruthers Corners. Nearby stood a mannequin authentically dressed like a Potawatomi

Indian, the indigenous people who had occupied the area before the settlers came. Across the room was a bronze bust of Col. Beauregard Hollingsworth Madison, one of the town's founders, a gift from his great-great-grandson. Other walls displayed rare maps, family portraits, landscape paintings, swords, muskets, and miscellaneous farm tools.

Impressive. Up till now, many of these items had resided in cardboard boxes, rusty file cabinets, and locked closets.

"It's fantastic," exclaimed Bootsie, this being the first time she'd seen the new wing. An opening for the public was scheduled during the upcoming Watermelon Days festival.

"I'll say," nodded Lizzie. "This looks like a real museum."

"It *is* a real museum," huffed Cookie, insulted by this misguided compliment.

"Oh, you know what I mean."

"This is going to be a showplace," interceded Bootsie, averting hurt feeling among her friends. "You must be very proud."

"It's certainly a change from the clutter of the past." Cookie smiled, brushing her dishwater blonde hair out of her eyes. She'd been working on the displays all morning, leaving her hot and sweaty.

"I wish Grammy were here to see this," said Aggie, concern clouding her blue eyes. Maddy's stroke had frightened her. Mortality isn't a subject most teens think about very much.

"Don't worry, your Grammy will be out of the hospital soon," Cookie assured the girl. "I promise I'll give her a special tour."

~ ~ ~

That same day Wanda Schaeffer was walking her dog along the edge of Never Ending Swamp. It was a small breed, a Chihuahua or Dachshund or maybe a Pomeranian. She used one of those retractable leashes, allowing the dog freedom to roam. That's how it came to find the bone.

We're not talking about a chicken bone. This was a human femur. The longest bone in the body, it's comprised of a diaphysis (shaft) and two epiphyses (extremities) that articulate with adjacent bones in the hip and knee. A thighbone, it's easy to recognize.

Wanda shrieked.

Then she took out her iPhone and called the police.

CHAPTER SEVEN

Low-Level Walking

Maddy used the remote gizmo to click off the TV mounted on the wall in front of her hospital bed. She had become bored with "My Family and Yours," one of the soap operas her friend Lizzie watched on a daily basis. "My stories," she called them.

Pulling the sheet back, Maddy swung her feet over the side of the bed. The hospital bed was elevated, so she had to carefully slide off the side until her feet touched the tile floor. Her legs seemed to wobble, as if they could barely support her weight. Not sure of her balance, she gripped the railing to steady herself. Oh my.

Maybe I was too rash, trying to get out of bed on my own, she told herself. *What if I fall on the tile and break my hip. I'll never recover. We know how that goes, old folks fading fast after receiving a traumatic injury.*

Just then a nurse stepped into the small private room, stopping mid-stride when she saw the patient out of bed. "Hold on, honey," she cautioned. "You may not be ready to go hiking yet."

"So I'm discovering."

The nurse took her by the arm. "Here, let me help you back into bed."

"I'd rather you help me walk. My physical therapist wants me to start getting some exercise. He says, 'Use it or lose it.'"

"Sounds like that jerk Morris." Morris Maxwell was a former Army drill sergeant who treated his physical therapy patients like boot camp recruits.

Maddy didn't recognize this particular nurse. She must be new to the shift. "Where's Natalie Thackeray?"

"Natalie doesn't come on till 7 o'clock. She's your night nurse."

"Oh, that's right." How had she forgotten that? Was her brain still scrambled from the stroke?

The woman in the starched white uniform said, "My name's Katherine – Katherine Meany. I usually work the second floor."

Maddy looked around, confused. "Which floor is this?"

"Third. Our rehabilitation units are on this floor. They moved you up here two days ago."

"Oh."

"Ready for that walk?" Katherine Meany guided her toward the door. "Stroke survivors need to start out with simple activities, such as low-level walking, self-care tasks, and mobility exercises. That avoids deconditioning of the muscles as well restores balance and coordination."

"Can we go down to the toxicology lab?"

"Why would you want to go to the labs?" the new nurse frowned. "Those are on the basement level."

Maddy shrugged, although it took some effort. "I'm just curious. Never been to a toxicology lab. We can take the elevator, can't we?"

~ ~ ~

Tilly was gathering up her mother's quilting supplies to take with her to the hospital later tonight. Burpyville Memorial had liberal visiting hours on the third floor where the recuperation unit was located. Problem was, she couldn't find the fabric scraps that her mother wanted to use along the quilt's border. They were probably mixed in the bins of material the women kept at the Hoosier Senior Recreational Center where the Quilters Club usually worked.

Tilly was running late, still having to fix dinner for her Dad, and didn't have time to make a side trip to the Center. What's more, this was her housekeeper's day off; Mrs. Grottman only came Mondays through Thursdays. Oh well, maybe there was enough here for her mother to fiddle with.

Tilly had never shared her mother's passion for needlecraft. That DNA trait must have skipped a generation, landing in her daughter Aggie's genetic makeup. What was that called? – Atavism.

Aggie was clever, like her grandmother. Able to solve complicated puzzles, made A's in English, ranked at the top of the Honor Roll. But she was awkward, all but failing her gymnastics class. Go figure the laws of Mendelian Inheritance!

After dinner, Tilly bundled up the quilting materials, gathered her kids, put on their jackets, tied their shoes, and piled the three of them into the family's Honda Odyssey. Off to the hospital.

CHAPTER EIGHT

The Death Scene

Police Chief Jim Purdue responded to the call. Deputy Pete Hitzer had been tied up with a fender-bender out on the Highway 21 Bypass. Deputy Evers Gochnauer was looking into a stolen car; there had been a rash of them lately. Wanda Shaeffer had sounded hysterical, so the chief climbed into the police cruiser, turned on the flashers, and headed out.

She had been walking her dog along the western edge of Never Ending Swamp, 400 acres of bog and primeval trees just north of Caruthers Corners on Highway 102. The Shaeffers lived near there, in a two-story farmhouse she had inherited from her parents. They had been small-time watermelon farmers, with 20 acres of fertile land. However, her husband Fat Karl wasn't a farmer; he worked as personnel manager at Wal-Mart down in Burpyville.

Chief Purdue examined the femur, wondering what a human bone was doing out here in the middle of nowhere. He'd had to park his Crown Vic and hike about a quarter mile down a narrow trail, most likely a deer path, to find her. Wanda explained how Pedro (it turned out the dog was a Mexican Chihuahua) had sniffed out the bone in those bushes over there.

The police chief pushed aside the leafy branches and used a stick to poke through the scattering of dead leaves. He turned up another bone, this one a tibia. Uh-oh.

Careful raking with the stick revealed more, a partial rib cage and a trowel-shaped shoulder blade. He had no doubt that a thorough combing of the area would produce an entire human skeleton.

Question remained, who was it? And how did he or she die?

~ ~ ~

Hopalong Cassidy didn't like what he read in this morning's newspaper about the death of a local doctor from radiation poisoning. It could mean only one thing: He was involved in a murder. Helping a shady guy – a spy maybe – pull off a little heist was one thing, but killing somebody was quite another. The first was good for jail time; the second could result in the death penalty.

Death row was located at the Federal Correctional Complex over in Terre Haut. Since the penalty was reinstated in 1977, three people had been executed by the Feds, including Timothy McVeigh, the guy who committed the Oklahoma City bombing. The state had executed another twenty.

Hoppy's future didn't look good.

~ ~ ~

The toxicology lab looked like a high school chemistry department – microscopes, Bunsen burners, glass beakers, and computer workstations. A couple of interns in white coats shuffled about the room, looking busy.

"There – satisfied?" said Nurse Meany.

Maddy looked around. "Who's in charge?"

"That would be Dr. Pettigrew," volunteered one of the interns. "He's down in the ICU flirting with Ginny Neuenschwander, that new Candy Striper."

"Harold!" his co-worker hissed, a warning to not be so forthcoming.

Maddy turned to Nurse Meany. "Can we go to the Intensive Care Unit?"

"Why do you want to see Felix Pettigrew?" she asked suspiciously.

"I told you: I'm interested in poisons."

CHAPTER NINE

Missing Persons

*T*illy was surprised that her mother wasn't in her hospital room. There was the empty bed, sheet rumpled, but no Madelyn Agnes Madison.

"Where's Grammy?" asked Aggie, brow furrowed.

"She – she's around here somewhere. Watch your sisters and I'll go check with the Third Floor Desk."

Aggie hustled her sisters Taylor and Mandy into the room, the quilting bundle in her arms. "I can't believe the hospital has lost my grandmother," she muttered under her breath. She was entering the Terrible Teens, a period of angst and unreasoned dissatisfaction.

Tilly raced down the hall to the nurse's station facing the elevator. "M-my mother, what have you done with my mother?" she sputtered.

"Who's your mother?" responded a bored-looking nurse's aid, glancing up from her *National Inquirer*. The headline blared: LIFE ON MARS DISCOVERED.

"Madelyn Madison, Room 312."

"Oh, she took the elevator with Nurse Meany. Probably went down to the cafeteria. Dinner menu tonight includes apple strudel. You go late it's all gone."

"Forget the strudel. Just give me my mother!"

~ ~ ~

Hoppy Casals tried to contact the mysterious man who paid him the fifty grand, but the phone number didn't work.

A message said it had been disconnected, but that couldn't be right. He had to locate this guy – Michael was his name.

Hoppy didn't know where the man lived but he'd once spotted him at Wal-Mart. Judging by the blue jacket Michael had been wearing, Hoppy figured he worked there.

Climbing into his battered old van – it still said HOPPY'S PLUMBING & REFRIGERATION on the side – he headed down Highway 21 toward Burpyville. He could feel the beads of sweat gathering on his forehead. Michael had better be there in Wal-Mart's Hardware Department or he'd be screwed. Nervously, he glanced in his rearview mirror to make sure no cops were following him. How did he get into this predicament?

Well, it started when he'd been approached by this Michael that day at Ivor Yokovich's house. Ivor had called him to fix a busted pipe in his basement, a small cottage over on Jinks Lane.

By the time he got there, the basement was flooded with two feet of water. It looked like an indoor swimming pool without a diving board. Fixing the broken pipe had taken less than twenty minutes, but he charged by the hour, a quick $125.

Ivor Yokovich had paid him in cash, but Hoppy noticed he had gotten the money from this guy Michael. His visitor was carrying a wad of cash the size of an overstuffed *pirozhok*.

Later Michael had taken him aside, saying he had a deal to discuss. It involved his former government work. The project had been classified Top Secret, but that had been so long ago who cared? He'd read somewhere that the US Air Force had discontinued the program, the last missile site deactivated in 1987.

Meeting in a Burpyville bar, the guy had offered him fifty grand to reveal a few secrets. That was more than Hoppy had made in a year as a small-town plumber.

He pulled into the Wal-Mart lot and parked near the entrance marked Home & Pharmacy. The Hardware Department was on this end of the superstore. Racing inside, he navigated the product-laden aisles, zigzagging over to the area that displayed power tools, hammers, saws, shop vacuums, and wrench sets. An octagonal-shaped counter was manned by a guy wearing a royal blue Wal-Mart vest. His nametag said Darryl.

"Excuse me," began Hoppy, "I'm looking for one of your associates who works here in the Hardware Department. A tall guy, dark hair, mole next to his upper lip, cleft chin. His name's Michael."

"Nobody named Michael works back here."

CHAPTER TEN

Chatting Up a Candy Striper

Dr. Felix Pettigrew was chatting up a blonde young enough to be his daughter. No doubt this was the estimable Ginny Neuenschwander. Dr. Pettigrew was leaning on a counter outside the ICU, a goofy grin on his face, watching as the Candy Striper rearranged books and magazines on her hospitality cart. Rather than the old red-and-white uniform, she wore a dark pleated skirt and blue polo shirt with the hospital's logo on it.

"Hi, Dr. Pettigrew –" Maddy began.

"Not now, I'm busy," he replied without diverting his gaze from the young blonde.

"Fine, I'll tell Ralph Niedermayer that you're too busy for patients." Niedermayer was president of the Hospital's board. She'd met him through Lizzie and Edgar. Lizzie's husband still served on the board of directors.

Suddenly Dr. Pettigrew gave Maddy his full attention. "How may I help you, madam?"

"I wanted to ask you about Dr. Kardashian's death. I understand you ran the toxicology report."

"I'm sorry, that information is confidential."

"No problem, I'll have Ralph get me the info." She wasn't really on a first-name basis with the board president, but Pettigrew didn't know that."

"What did you want to know?" he continued smoothly, now as helpful as the Information Desk at the Public

Library. "Perhaps I can save you the bother of talking with Mr. Niedermayer."

"Thank you. Dr. K was my vascular neurologist, you see. Perhaps you can understand my concern over his untimely death."

"Yes, it was a shock for us all. He was well liked around the hospital."

Nurse Meany was hanging back, trying to avoid getting caught up in inner-hospital politics. She seemed to have developed an intense interest in one of the books on Ginny Neuenschwander's hospitality cart, a tome titled *Savage Love Lost*.

"I understand his death may not have been from natural causes."

"What makes you say that? I don't believe any findings have been released yet."

Maddy smiled. "Today's *Burpyville Gazette* said the police suspected foul play." She had him there. *Now let's see him wiggle out of that*, she thought.

"I haven't seen today's paper. Busy schedule, you know."

Maddy glanced at the Candy Striper, then back to him. "I'm sure," she said.

"I can't go into details, but we did find an abnormality in the toxicology screening."

"Poison?"

"Not *per se*."

"Then a drug overdose?"

"Not that either."

"What then?"

Pettigrew gave her a condescending smile. "You wouldn't understand the technical details. We found a

44

slight trace of an element known as polonium-210 in his system. It can be fatal. Now if you'll excuse me, I have work to do." He turned back to the Candy Striper, the goofy smile returning to his face.

~ ~ ~

"There you are, Mom!" Tilly Tidemore encountered her missing mother in the elevator lobby on the basement level. Tilly had ridden down floor-by-floor searching for the wayward patient.

"We were just getting exercise," Nurse Meany replied quickly, not about to be blamed for Maddy's unplanned excursion. "Her physical therapist recommended that she do slow-walks."

"We were worried," sighed Tilly. "Aggie and the girls are waiting up in your room. I brought that quilting stuff, but I'm not sure I got everything. I wish you'd take up a simpler hobby – like playing bridge."

"I never did like card games," Maddy rolled her eyes. This facial dexterity was a good sign. There seemed to be no paralysis of her facial muscles. Her speech was returning to normal.

"You used to play Old Maids with me when I was a girl."

"That's what mothers do. I wouldn't choose to do it as a recreational pastime on my own time."

"Mom!"

"Help me into the elevator. I'm ready to crawl back into my hospital bed."

Balanced between the nurse and her daughter, Maddy rode back to the Third Floor where Aggie was trying to keep her sisters occupied. The girls were more than a decade younger than Aggie, so her interaction was more akin to a babysitter than a big sister. She preferred spending time with friends at school or her cousin N'yen in Chicago. Or the Quilters Club.

"Grammy," she squealed with excitement when Maddy entered the room.

"Hi there, Aggie," came the tired response. She was eager to get beneath the sheet. Her excursion had taken more out of her than she'd expected. She felt like an old woman.

"Okay, Mom, into bed," ordered Tilly. The nurse stood back, willing to let the daughter take charge.

"Do you want your quilting supplies?" asked Aggie, holding up the bulky bundle.

"I think I'll wait till tomorrow to tackle that."

Tilly tucked her mother under the sheet. "How long are you going to be in this prison, Mom?"

"Hard to say. I'm over the medical part. This is the rehab unit."

"A few more days, then we'll send her home," offered Nurse Meany. "She's making good progress."

Maddy hated being discussed as if she weren't there, but held her tongue. Everybody meant well. It was funny how illness seems to render you invisible as a sentient being. "Aggie, did you bring your iPhone?" she prompted.

"Got it right here."

"Will you look something up for me – on Google or Wikipedia or whatever."

"Okay." The girl had pulled out her Smartphone and moved closer to the bed. "What do you want me to find?"

"Polonium-210."

"Poly-what?"

Maddy repeated the name.

"Mom, what on earth?" said Tilly.

"It's something she heard downstairs," said Katherine Meany.

Aggie typed onto the iPhone's screen, using her thumbs. "Here it is. Says it's a chemical element with the Atomic Number of 84, an unstable radioactive metal with a short half-life."

"Radioactive?" said Tilly, looking at the nurse.

Nurse Meany shrugged as if to disavow any knowledge of this substance.

"Fascinating," muttered Maddy Madison.

Aggie continued reading from her tiny screen. "Says here, polonium was discovered in 1898 by Marie and Pierre Curie when they chemically separated it out of uranium ore."

"A nice footnote for your science class," teased her grandmother. Science was not one of Aggie's strongest subjects.

"Why are you interested in polonium?" asked Aggie.

"It may have been used to kill Dr. Kardashian."

"Your neurologist?" said Tilly.

"Yes, I just learned that Dr. K's toxicology report showed a trace of polonium-210."

Nurse Meany looked uncomfortable, having just put the two conversations together.

Aggie continued reading from her iPhone: "Wikipedia says, 'Its intense radioactivity makes it dangerously toxic to life.'"

"Wasn't that what the Russians used to kill that KGB defector?" said Maddy, wishing Cookie were here to confirm this factoid. Cookie Bentley was known for her near-eidetic memory.

"What defector?" said Tilly.

"I'll look it up," volunteered Aggie.

CHAPTER ELEVEN

Searching for Bones

Chief Purdue and his two deputies carefully worked the crime scene. The coroner was there too, but he was just a local doctor who was on-call for any cases involving violent, sudden, or suspicious deaths. A rare occurrence in Caruthers County.

Deputy Hitzer had wrapped up that fender-bender, ticketing a local teen. Deputy Gochnauer reported the stolen car had been another case of joyriding. The Mustang turned up six blocks away.

After an hour or two, the remaining pieces of the skeleton were found, with a few exceptions – probably the result of foraging animals. The skull was smooth and round, the eye sockets seeming to stare accusatively. The adult human has 206 bones in all; they had recovered 189.

The coroner pulled a tape measure from his black bag and measured the length of one of the femurs. He did a quick calculation and announced, "This man was 5-foot-11."

"How do you know it was a gent?" asked Petie Hitzer.

"The hips. They're different between men and women."

"And how can you be sure how tall he was?" Evers Gochnauer wanted to know.

"The length of the femur is on average about 27% of a person's height," Doc Medford replied. "Simple math."

"What killed him?" asked the police chief.

"A bullet to the brain. Before you ask, there's a neat hole

in the back of the skull. Looks like it was administered execution style. So it was probably some kind of punishment."

"What color eyes did he have?"

"I'm not that good," laughed the Doc.

~ ~ ~

"C'mon," insisted Hopalong Cassidy. "I'm sure a guy named Michael works here in the Hardware Department. I've seen him here."

"Sorry to burst your bubble, but I've worked here the past two years and we've never had anyone named Michael in this department."

"I'm telling you –"

"Tell it to the hand, buddy." But the part of his hand Darryl exhibited consisted of only one finger.

"Let me talk to your boss."

"My supervisor's out sick today. You got any complaint, take it to the front office."

Hoppy scowled. "I'll do just that."

~ ~ ~

Beau Madison dropped by the Mayor's Office. Sometimes he missed it, being Mayor, overseeing the town's business. But now his son-in-law held that position, which was next best thing to having the job himself.

Mark Tidemore – A/K/A Mark the Shark – was a former lawyer married to Beau's daughter Tilly. A hometown boy, he'd done a stint in a high-powered law firm in Los Angeles, but had returned to Caruthers Corners with Tilly and their daughter Agnes. Now they had two more, Taylor and Mandy.

Beau was proud of Tilly's brothers. Bill was a social

services worker in Chicago who helped kids. Freddie was the Caruthers Corners Fire Chief. But if he were to be honest, he felt closest to Mark the Shark.

Maybe it was because they had both sat in the mayor's seat. Maybe it was because they both loved Tilly. Or maybe it was because Mark would stop at nothing when it came to doing the right thing. He admired that kind of integrity.

The town was growing under Mark Tidemore's stewardship, the population increasing as new businesses came in. The new Industrial Park was filling up.

"The trick," Mark liked to say, "is growing without getting too big. We want to preserve the small-town values that make Caruthers Corners such a pleasant place to live."

So far, he'd kept that balance.

Beau liked to drop in to see Mark at the end of the workday. Sometimes thirteen-year-old Aggie would join them and the trio would stroll down to the Dairy Queen for a vanilla custard (as folks called soft-serve ice cream around here).

Today, Beau just felt lonely. With Maddy being in the hospital, he felt like Vincent Price in *The Last Man on Earth*, surrounded by zombies, no human companionship to be had. This stroke had scared him. He didn't know what he'd do without his wife of more than thirty-five years. What if she didn't recover? What if he had to put her in a nursing home?

"Hi, Dad," Mark Tidemore greeted him. The secretary already gone for the day, Beau had walked right in as was his usual custom.

"Hello, Mr. Mayor." The formality a joke between them. "How's Mom?"

"Talked with her by phone earlier. She's sounding better. Less slurring of the speech."

"That's good news. Sometimes full faculties return, given time."

"So the doctor says. Maddy's new doctor, that is. A neurologist by the name of Blatt. Don't know him, but he's highly recommended. From the same medical center as Dr. Kardashian."

"What a shame about Dr. Kardashian, dropping dead in the hospital parking lot."

"Maddy's got a bee in her bonnet that he was murdered."

"That's highly unlikely. He was well liked, a pillar of the community over in Burpyville. I've been on several countywide committees with him. Nice guy. Hard to believe anybody would have it out for him."

"Yes, I agree Maddy's off-base on this one. But maybe it's good that she's looking for more mysteries to solve. I see that as a sign of recovery."

Mark chuckled. The Quilters Club's sleuthing was kind of a family joke – although the gals *had* solved a number of local crimes. Couldn't take that away from them. "I'll ask Jim Purdue to touch base with Chief Crenshaw over in Burpyville to get the real score. I heard they were running a routine toxicology screening on Dr. Kardashian. Results are probably back by now. There was some talk of food poisoning. He had an exotic palate, I'm told. Ate odder things than that guy Anthony Bourdain on 'Parts Unknown.'"

"I've seen that CNN program. He travels all over the world eating squid brains and the like. Not for me. I'll stick with pork tenderloin and watermelon pie."

"I'll let you know what Jim hears from Crenshaw," Mark said. But he knew Jim Purdue would probably tell Beau first. The two had been best friends since high school. Jim the quarterback on the football team; Beau the high scorer on the basketball court. The past few years, the Purdues and Madisons even vacationed together, Walt Disney World and fun places like that. Last year Aggie had gone with them.

Beau said, "You know, Jim and I went to school with Frank Crenshaw. He's from here. Moved to Burpyville after high school. A good man."

"I'm sure he'll get to the bottom of this Kardashian business – tell us whether it was foul play or simply a bad oyster."

"Yeah," Beau chuckled. "If the Quilters Club doesn't beat him to it."

CHAPTER TWELVE

Russian Assassins

"You think the Russians killed Dr. Kardashian?" said Bootsie, astonished. She and the other members of the Quilters Club were gathered around Maddy's hospital bed.

"I didn't say that. I said the Russians used the same radioactive material to kill that guy in London ten years ago. Alexander Litvinenko was his name. I had Aggie look it up on Wikipedia."

"Was that the fellow who got stabbed with an umbrella?" asked Lizzie. The redhead was not one who paid close attention to the news.

"No, the umbrella was used on a dissident writer by the Bulgarians. They killed him on Waterloo Bridge using an umbrella with a hidden pneumatic mechanism that injected a poison called risin," corrected Cookie, her encyclopedic memory at work.

"But I heard the Russians assisted the Bulgarians on that one," said Bootsie. She watched the History Channel. It had been carrying a lot of spy programs lately. "Declassified," stuff like that.

"Maybe so," said Maddy. "But I'm talking about a guy the Russians killed using polonium-210."

"Never heard of it," said Lizzie. The redhead had not excelled in her chemistry classes in high school. And she'd avoided science classes altogether in college. It bored her.

"Point is, Dr. K was murdered using the same radioactive poison. We need to find out who did it."

"Why do we have to be the ones to do it?" grumbled Lizzie. "Let's leave it to Burpyville's police chief to solve. Isn't that what Frank Crenshaw gets paid to do?"

"You don't have the same attitude when it comes to Bootsie's husband," accused Maddy.

"That's closer to home. And we're helping out her hubby."

"Jim doesn't usually want our help," smiled Bootsie.

"But we give it to him anyway," added Maddy.

"What's so important about this Murder-She-Wrote mystery?" whined Lizzie.

"The reason we want to find this killer is because Dr. K saved my life," Maddy put it bluntly. "You'd be talking to a vegetable right now if he had not been on hand."

"Lizzie may have a point," cautioned Cookie. "We don't usually get involved with murders. And this one could be dangerous, especially if radioactivity is involved. I don't want to mess with polonium-210. I'd just as soon handle a rattlesnake."

"What about that last case?" responded Maddy. "A man was trying to murder the whole town with botulism."

"True," admitted Bootsie. "That maniac killed Herbert Hoople and was going to poison the entire town's water supply." Hoople was one of the famous quadruples.

"But why us?" repeated Lizzie. Just being cranky.

Aggie hadn't spoken up this entire time. This was a Saturday, so she'd been able to ride over to Burpyville Memorial with them. "But we're detectives," insisted the girl. "This is what we do."

~ ~ ~

That morning Dan Sokolowski, owner of Dan's Den of Antiquity, had received a delivery of new merchandise. Well, old merchandise to be accurate. After all, this was an antiques shop.

Last weekend he'd made a field trip up to the big flea market in Swisstown, a wide place in the road near the Michigan border. This swap meet was the largest "industry" in the area. People came from all over with their goods – distressed furniture, knick knacks and porcelain figurines, baked apple pies, wooden handicrafts, homemade peach preserves, used tools, sourwood honey, old toys, secondhand dresses, and assorted antiques salvaged from attics. Dan always made decent finds there. And the prices were reasonable, allowing him a fair markup for resale in Dan's Den of Antiquity. He did a good business with travelers stopping in Caruthers Corners on their way to Indianapolis.

As a practice, he hired a Swisstown man with a truck to deliver all his purchases in one load. Today's delivery contained several interesting items: a circa 1910 oak half-and-half, an Amish reclaimed barn-wood coffee table, a Victorian press-back doll cradle, matching Barbola Rose Harp table lamps, a working Stewart Wagner tube radio, assorted walking canes (one with a hidden sword), two large Chinese Foo Dogs carved from soapstone, an early 1900s MacDougall Hoosier State cupboard, a Louis XVI satinwood dresser, a painting of a former Indiana senator, three pocket watches with 14k gold-filled cases, assorted jewelry, and an 1880s white-on-white Wedding Quilt. Not a bad haul.

Tom the deliveryman and his halfwit brother unloaded the items from the truck and carried them into the shop. Past 80, Dan Sokolowski avoided heavy lifting. He'd had a bad back for years. Strained it playing croquet at a church picnic.

"Thanks for the help," Sokolowski waved goodbye to the two men.

"See you next month," acknowledged Tom. He had the antiques dealer's schedule down pat – a regular customer. When Tom and his brother weren't delivering things in their truck, they worked as "haulers," sort of like a civilian taxi service for Amish who didn't drive.

Dan Sokolowski walked around his shop examining the new pieces one-by-one, checking for dings, running his hand over polished wood, admiring the craftsmanship. He was particularly pleased with the Hoosier State cupboard. People liked to find Indiana antiques in his shop.

It was indeed a fine piece of cabinetry. G.P. McDougall & Son of Frankfort, Indiana, made nice kitchen cabinets back in their day. This piece dated back to the 1920s. Unlike most cupboards, the tambor roll on this one pulled upward and latched into place. He liked to find them this way; the old finish over top of the oak. The porcelain countertop was in nice shape too. And the original McDougall logo was proudly displayed at the top center. Likely he could get $3,000 for the piece; he had paid half that amount for it.

As he passed by the table where he kept quilts stacked, he paused to admire the newly acquired Wedding Quilt. Probably Amish, judging by its stark simplicity. Slightly off white, it measured 87" x 76". Hand stitched at 7-8, its grid work featured tiny squares. A quilted four-chain link pattern formed the border. He noticed some very light binding wear, and on the front there was a tiny rip, a surface tear about ½" long. But with this kind of densely quilted handwork, he figured it would easily fetch $200. He'd got it for $20.

All in all, a good haul. Now to catalog the items and enter them into his database. Dan Sokolowski appeared to be a simple octogenarian immigrant from Germany, but in his office sat a Microsoft **Commercial Surface Book with a Performance Base - 1TB / Intel Core i7** running Oracle's MySQL, a high-end relational database management system (RDBMS). He might be an antiques dealer but he didn't live in the past.

CHAPTER THIRTEEN

Nuclear Theory

*T*hat afternoon Maddy telephoned the Physics Department at Indiana University down in Bloomington. Aggie had Googled the phone number for her. According to the website it was a medium-sized department, composed of 38 professors and about 100 grad students. It offered studies in particle physics, astrophysics, cosmology, condensed matter physics, accelerator physics, and nuclear physics.

She asked to speak with Dr. Fitzwilliam in the Nuclear Theory Center. There was a pause, a slight wrangling with his secretary, and then the professor came on the line.

"How might I help you?" said Roger Fitzwilliam, Ph.D., M.A.T., M.S. His bio on the website had identified him as a nuclear physicist.

"I hope you don't think I'm some nut trying to make an atomic bomb in my basement, but how difficult is it to get some polonium-210?"

The phone went silent for a moment.

"Extremely difficult, I'd say. It's very rare in nature because of the short half-life of its isotopes. It can be found in uranium ores at about 0.1 mg per metric ton. Not worth harvesting because applications for polonium are pretty sparse. Besides, its intense radioactivity makes it highly dangerous."

"But surely it has some use."

"Polonium was a critical part of the Fat Man bomb dropped on Nagasaki in 1945. Polonium and beryllium were key ingredients in the detonator at the center of the bomb's plutonium pit. That fact was classified until the 1960s."

"Oh my. I was just kidding about making an atomic bomb."

"I wasn't too worried. To make polonium requires a cyclotron to bombard bismuth with protons or deuterons. You don't happen to have a cyclotron in your basement, do you?"

"I don't even know what a cyclotron is," she admitted.

Dr. Fitzwilliam chuckled on the other end of the line. "A cyclotron is a type of particle accelerator. It uses electrical power to accelerate charged particles in a spiral path. The collision of those particles produces certain radioactive isotopes."

"Hm, all I have is a Cuisinart."

"I doubt that will do the trick. You can see why polonium is exceedingly rare. Only about 100 grams are produced each year, practically all of it in Russia."

"Wasn't polonium-210 used to assassinate that Russian diplomat in London about ten years ago?"

"Oh, you're referring to the poisoning of Alexander Litvinenko. That's credited as being the first recorded death by polonium. But it very likely killed Madam Curie's daughter who was exposed to it in a lab accident. She developed leukemia."

"My granddaughter told me Madam Curie discovered polonium."

"Yes, in 1898. She named it after her native country, Poland."

"How sure are British authorities that the Russians killed that defector?"

"Very sure. The polonium used in Litvinenko's death came from a nuclear facility in the city of Sarov, 450 miles southeast of Moscow."

Maddy wasn't satisfied. "Couldn't it have come from somewhere else?"

"Not likely. The Soviet's Avangard plant was the only place in the world producing polonium at that time. The US and other countries stopped making it in the 1970s. You can't store polonium. In 138 days it turns to lead."

"How was he poisoned?"

"Two Russian agents fed it to him in a cup of tea. They left a radioactive trail a mile wide while making three trips to London in their attempt to feed Litvinenko the liquid polonium."

"It has to be ingested?"

"Polonium-210 is poisonous only once it has entered the body. Therefore it either has to be swallowed, breathed, or introduced through broken skin."

Maddy thought of the scratch on Dr. K's arm. "Is death instantaneous?"

"Oh no. This is radiation poisoning. Death can take hours or even weeks, depending on the amount of exposure."

"How much polonium's needed to kill someone?"

"Just a few micrograms. Polonium is one of the most toxic substances known to humankind. It's 250 billion times more toxic than cyanide."

~ ~ ~

Dan Sokolowski was inspecting the Amish Wedding Quilt he'd bought at the flea market in Swisstown. It was a fine piece. Too bad about the ½" tear on the surface of the quilt. Perhaps it could be mended. A good seamstress could make the imperfection almost invisible, he told himself.

The antique dealer picked up the telephone, an old rotary instrument, and dialed the seven-digit number for the Ridenour residence. He remembered when telephone numbers were only three digits long and you shared a party line with other patrons.

He listened to the phone ring on the other end. Elizabeth Kay Ridenour was the best hand at sewing in the entire town. She'd won the Watermelon Days quilting competition two or three times. If anyone could fix that tiny tear it was the banker's redheaded wife.

~ ~ ~

Aggie was on her iPhone, talking with her cousin N'yen. He'd promised to come down for Watermelon Days. The festival would be getting underway in less than a week.

"My Mom and Dad have to work," the eleven-year-old boy was saying. "They can't drive me down. I'm trying to convince them to let me take the bus. There's only one stop between Chicago and there. I've done it lots of times before."

"I sure hope you can come. My Crazy Quilt is entered in the competition. Well, in the junior division of the competition."

"What could you win?"

"A trophy."

"I'd rather win money myself. I'd use it to buy me a **Nintendo** Wii U gaming system."

"Don't you already have a Wii?"

"The old model. But it only has 512MB of internal flash memory. The new Wii U comes with 32GB, plus it'll support external hard drives. And it uses an IBM multi-core processor."

"You don't need a new gaming system. Your old one works perfectly fine," she told her cousin.

"Do too."

"Oh, spend your money on whatever you like. I don't really care. But let me know if you're coming down or not."

CHAPTER FOURTEEN

Complaint Department

Karl Schaeffer was about to call it a day when the grubby little guy with wild, spiky hair burst into the office. *Good grief*, he thought. *Not another complainer. I need to get home.*

His wife had phoned him to tell him about the human bones Pedro had unearthed. That dog could sniff out a scrap of food in an empty kitchen. Wanda sounded pretty shaken up. He needed to go home and comfort her, give her a hug, ply her with a stiff drink. Matter of fact, he wouldn't mind one himself.

The man who had just walked in the door looked angry, his eyebrows knitted, mouth like an upside down U. It got so you could tell a problem customer by his body language, a carper who couldn't be satisfied no matter what concessions you offered him.

"I wanna see somebody in charge," the man demanded. Maybe 5-foot-4, he was as short as Karl was wide.

Fat Karl sighed resignedly. "Well, it's past five. I'm the only one left in the office, so I'll have to do. Tell me, what's your problem?"

"That guy Darryl in the Hardware Department is rude and unhelpful."

"I'm sorry to hear that. Please accept Wal-Mart's apology." There, that should do it ... but he knew more was coming.

"I need to get in touch with one of your employees, but your guy Darryl claims he doesn't work here. I've seen him back there in the Hardware Department with my own eyes. That Darryl's blowing smoke at me."

Fat Karl's job description was Assistant Manager – a catchall term that included Personnel Department, Human Resources, and (mostly) Payroll. "Who's this gentleman you're trying to locate? If he works here, I'll have his name in my computer," said the roly-poly man.

"Michael."

"Michael what?"

"Dunno. Michael's the name I know him by."

"And he works in Hardware?"

"Right. It's really important I reach him."

Fat Karl typed the name into his computer, added a Department Code. "Nope, there's no Michael assigned to Hardware. We've got one in the Pharmacy Department. Another in Electronics."

"No, Hardware."

"Sorry, no Michael. Got a Mikhail."

"A what?"

"Mikhail. I think that may be Russian for Michael."

"Maybe I misheard him. What's his full name?"

Fat Karl hesitated. "We don't give out personal information about employees."

The man looked like he was going to blow a gasket. "I'm not asking personal information – just his name."

"Well, I guess we could give you that much. It's Mikhail Kuzmich. Says here he's originally from the Republic of Azerbaijan. Huh, I thought he was from Russia."

"Yes, that sounds like the guy. He had an accent. How

can I get in touch with him?"

Fat Karl Schaeffer shook his head. "Can't help you there."

"What good does it do me to know his name but not how to find him?"

"Look, I've gotta go home. My wife found a dead body behind the house."

CHAPTER FIFTEEN

A Mob Hit

It was almost dark when the police wrapped up their work at the crime scene. Heading back to town, they left the area marked off with yellow tape. It wouldn't keep away curious farm boys, but perhaps a few deer would be fenced out.

Doc Medford hauled away the collection of bones, a near complete skeleton. The skull was perfectly preserved, except for the bullet hole in the external occipital ridge at the rear. Unquestionably murder. A suicide could never get a weapon into that position.

Twenty minutes later Police Chief Jim Purdue settled behind his desk, with his deputies facing him in chairs. His office was located at the right front of the police station. Two holding cells were found in back; they were empty tonight.

"Thanks for putting in the extra hours," he said to Pete Hitzer. The day shift had ended and he was now on his own time. The Chief nodded to Evers Gochnauer. "You too." Evers had come in early this afternoon. Yes, this investigation was going to clock up some overtime.

"No problem, Chief."

"Whatever you need, Boss."

Chief Purdue cleared his throat, staring down at a sketch he'd made of the crime scene, numbers representing the position of each scattered bone. "Any ideas on this?" he asked the men.

Petie was quicker than his fellow deputy. "Bullet in the back of the head. Execution style. That suggests it's mob related. They must've brought the vic out here in the sticks to do the hit far away from Indianapolis."

Evers nodded. "An execution means somebody's being punished for crossing the mob. I'd check with Indy to see if any *caporegime*s have disappeared in the last month or so."

"Why a *capo*?" the Chief asked.

"Well, the disappearance of anybody higher up the food chain – a *consigliere* or an underboss – would have been obvious by now. And anybody lower – a soldier – wouldn't be worth the two-hour drive from Circle City."

Evers Gochnauer's logic was sound. He might be slow, but he was sure. It would be a hard decision when it came time to pick his successor from between the two men. He had two other deputies, but they were only part-timers.

"Why not call that Feebie you know – Neil the Nailer. He could tell us what's going on with the Indy mob," suggested Petie Hitzer. "Maybe there's been some shifting in the hierarchy of the crews."

"Neil Wannamaker," the Chief identified the FBI Special Agent. "He's likely to swoop in here and take over the investigation. Wouldn't want that. At least not yet."

"Better him than those batty women," said Deputy Gochnauer. Evers didn't have a very high opinion of the Quilters Club, but he was smart enough not to go too far in expressing his opinion, being that Chief Purdue's wife was one of them.

"Okay, I'll give Neil a call first thing in the morning. Not much more we can do here tonight. I want to get home. My wife's holding dinner. Petie, you go home too. Evers, hold down the fort."

~ ~ ~

Fat Karl Schaeffer was late getting home for dinner, thanks to that jerk who had barged into his office at the end of the day, wanting the name of one of Wal-Mart's employees. If the guy had been less rude, he might have told him Mikhail Kuzmich had resigned two weeks ago. Said he was moving to California. He left no forwarding address. Sales people came and went, given the low wages and long hours.

Wanda was still distraught over finding the human remains. Pedro (the Chihuahua) was distraught over not getting to keep the bone. And Fat Karl was distraught that his dinner wasn't ready.

A big man weighing in at close to 300 pounds, Fat Karl needed a lot of fuel to keep going. He normally ate four to five meals a day. Plus snacks. He sat on a bench behind his desk, his butt too big for an office chair.

The average sumo wrestler weighs about 325 pounds. Fat Karl was well under that limit. But he thought he had something in common with those Japanese athletes. As the town's watermelon-eating champion, he considered his physique to be similar.

"Was the dead person a man or a woman?" he asked his wife.

"I don't know. It was just a pile of bones."

"Didn't the police make a determination?"

"If so, they didn't tell me."

Fat Karl waddled into the kitchen. "Got any pie?" he called to his wife, still in the living room. For his convenience, he'd had the front door, kitchen door and bedroom door widened. He slept alone on a king-size bed; Wanda slept in the next room. Perhaps that's why they had no children, just the Chihuahua.

"Outta watermelon pie, but got some blueberry and pumpkin."

"Good. I'll have one while I'm waiting for dinner."

~ ~ ~

Hopalong Cassidy drove back to Caruthers Corners, but didn't go straight home. Instead, Hoppy took Second Avenue, then cut over to Jinks Lane. He parked his van under the leafy oak in Ivor Yokovich's yard and tooted his horn.

The old man came to his door and looked out at the visitor. "What do you want?" he called. "I paid you for your plumbing."

Hoppy leaned out the van's window. "I need to get in touch with your friend Michael"

"Who?"

"Mikhail, whatever you call him. I need to reach him right away."

Ivor Yokovich waved his hand. "Go away," he said. "I do not know this person."

"Sure you do. I met him here. He hired me to do a job for him."

"That is your business, not mine. Go away."

Hoppy was losing his patience. First the Hardware Department guy, then the Wal-Mart manager, now this old coot Yokovich. He said, "You don't tell me where to find Mikhail, you're going to be talking to the FBI. I think he killed somebody."

CHAPTER SIXTEEN

The Irradiator in Mayapuri

When the night nurse came on duty, Maddy pressed the button that made the bed elevate her to a sitting position. "Natalie, I'm glad to see you. I need your help with something."

Nurse Thackeray placed the dinner tray on the overbed table and slid it in front of the patient. "Dinner is served," she said, ignoring the greeting.

"Yes, yes, I'll eat. But I need to talk with a doctor who understands the effects of radiation poisoning."

"Out of my league. I can direct you to a pediatrician or a cardiovascular surgeon or a gastroenterologist, but I have no idea who would know anything about radiation poisoning."

"How about a radiologist? Don't they use radioactive materials?"

"Sure, they use radium, radon, cobalt-60, iridium-192 – but for imaging. They're closer to being photographers than medical doctors, you ask me. They don't treat people for radioactive poisoning."

Then Maddy had another brainstorm. "How about an oncologist? They use radiation to treat cancer, don't they?"

"They use it as a tool. They don't try to cure its effects."

Maddy was stumped. "Then who?"

"This is a small hospital," said Natalie Thackeray. "We don't have doctors here who specialize in diagnostic radiology or nuclear medicine."

"Any ideas?"

"Well, maybe one."

~ ~ ~

"I'd like you to meet Dr. Madhuk Kapoor," said Nurse Thackeray. "He's new to our hospital staff."

"Pleased to meet you, I am sure," the man bowed. "Nurse says I might be of help in answering some questions for you."

Maddy looked confused. "Do you mind my asking your medical specialty?"

"I practice internal medicine," he replied, not expecting her questions to be so easy.

"I'm sorry to waste your time." She glanced reproachfully toward the nearby nurse. "I was looking for an expert in radiation poisoning."

"Why? Do you have symptoms?"

"No, not me. I'm just ... curious."

Nurse Thackeray stepped forward. "Dr. Kapoor comes to us from a hospital in New Delhi. He helped treat victims of the Mayapuri incident."

"What incident?" asked Maddy. She was thinking she should watch BBC more often.

Dr. Kapoor said, "In 2010 an AECL Gammacell 220 research irradiator belonging to Delhi University was sold for scrap metal. A dealer in Mayapuri dismantled the machine, unaware of its hazardous nature. The cobalt-60 source was cut into eleven pieces. One gentleman kept a small fragment in his wallet, two fragments went to a nearby shop, and the remaining eight stayed in the scrapyard. As a result, eight people were hospitalized with

Acute Radiation Syndrome. I helped treat them. Unfortunately, one died."

"Oh, so you do have experience with radiation poisoning."

"Sadly, madam, I do."

"And he'll be happy to answer your questions," interjected the nurse. "But don't take up too much of Dr. Kapoor's time. He has rounds to make."

CHAPTER SEVENTEEN

ARS

*T*he symptoms of Acute Radiation Syndrome (ARS) – also known as radiation poisoning, radiation sickness, or radiation toxicity – present themselves within 24 hours of exposure. Radiation damages DNA and other molecular structures within the cells. This degradation affects the cells' ability to divide normally. Symptoms can begin within one or two hours and may last for several months.

"Relatively smaller doses result in nausea and vomiting," Dr. Kapoor explained. "Another sign is a falling white cell blood count. Larger exposures can result in neurological effects and rapid death."

"How quickly can one die from radiation poisoning?"

"Alas, it depends on the level of radiation and time of exposure," he fluttered his hands to indicate no simple answer.

Maddy persisted. "What about an extremely high level?"

"Radiation exposure in the thousands of rems is fatal, though death usually comes after a day or two of intense nausea, headaches, fever, seizures, etc. Faster? A used fuel bundle puts out 10,000-20,000 rems per hour depending on how old they are. In all likelihood, that level would be instantly fatal."

~ ~ ~

Mark Tidemore phoned the police chief. "Jim, would you do me a favor and ride out to that old weather observation facility on Far Fields Road with a buddy of mine. I'd consider it a personal favor. Richie has bought some land out there in a government auction, but says when he went out there yesterday to inspect the property some Men in Black warned him away."

"Men in Black? You mean like Tommy Lee Jones and Will Smith?"

"Probably more like a private security firm that hasn't got word of the sale yet."

"No problem. Where do I find your friend?"

"He's down at the Town Hall with me. Likes to keep a low profile."

"What is he, a movie star or something?"

"Exactly," said the mayor.

~ ~ ~

Word came from Chicago that N'yen would be coming down for an end-of-summer visit. Bill and Amanda had booked him a seat on the Trailways that stops over in Indy. As usual, he would be staying with his Grammy and Grampy. He always got Bill's old room.

That meant he'd get to ride the fire truck with his Uncle Freddie in the Watermelon Days parade, go fishing with Grampy and Uncle Edgar, play video games with Aggie, and hang out with the Quilters Club. He liked being a detective.

He considered himself the luckiest boy in the world to have been adopted into the Madison family. He had the best of both worlds, pride in his Asian heritage and a sense of belonging with this welcoming Indiana dynasty. *R□t may m□n*, as he would say in Vietnamese. Very lucky.

CHAPTER EIGHTEEN

Special Ops

itch Richardson was indeed a handsome man, just as People Magazine had proclaimed on its cover ("Handsome Hitch Picked As Sexiest Man Alive"). Chief Purdue was a little intimidated by the man's perfect features: the straight nose, bright white teeth, azure blue eyes, and the mantle of wavy blond hair.

Jim Purdue once had wavy hair, but that was many years ago. Now his bald pate was covered by a policeman's cap. He had a noticeable paunch, slumping shoulders, and slightly bowed legs. In other words, Jim looked nothing like the movie star sitting next to him in the passenger seat of his Crown Vic.

Far Fields Road was narrow and unpaved, more a thin line on a map than a true thoroughfare. It led nowhere, dead-ending at the old weather station. A car couldn't even get that far because a security gate blocked the road. A 40-acre plot had been sectioned off with 20-guage galvanized-steel chain-link fencing. Razor wire ran along the top. Seemed like pretty tight security for a far-flung weather station.

When Chief Purdue eased the cruiser up to the gate, bumper practically touching the chain link, he was surprised to see two men in dark military garb emerge from the bushes on the other side.

"May we help you?" one of the men greeted them. He

was carrying a 9mm Heckler & Koch MP5K. Its slightly curved steel magazine had a 30-round capacity. The submachine gun could fire 900 rounds per minute. A lot of firepower for simple guard duty.

Jim Purdue got out of the car and walked up to the fence. He noted both military men wore the rank of lieutenant. Each man's sleeve displayed a badge-shaped patch labeled AIR FORCE SPECIAL OPERATION COMMAND. What was Special Ops doing out here?

"Howdy, boys," he greeted them. "What brings you out to this neck of the woods?"

"That's privileged information, sir. We'll have to ask you to turn back. This is a secure area."

The police chief took off his cap to scratch his head, as if considering their words. "'Fraid you boys got it backwards. This is private property owned by the gentleman seated in my cruiser. You're the ones trespassing. I'm going to have to ask *you* to leave."

The Special Ops men raised their weapons slightly. "We can't do that, sir. We have our orders."

"If you're refusing a lawful order of a police officer, I'll have to place you under arrest."

"You can't do that, sir. We have authority here."

"Got any papers to prove it?" He looked from man to man. "I thought not. Well, I have papers here showing this gentleman is the legal owner of the property. I'm ordering you to put down those weapons and exit the property."

"Let's see your papers."

Chief Purdue handed the bill of sale to the closest Special Op, sliding them through the crack between gate and chain-link fence.

The two men huddled over the papers, then looked up. "We're going to have to call in for clarification of our orders," he said.

"Okay, I'll wait."

~ ~ ~

Mikhail Kuzmich flew in from California for this meeting. The plumber had become a problem. He should have tied up this loose end after the man served his purpose. But he would remedy that now.

The Azerbaijani sat across from Harry "Hopalong Cassidy" Casals at Café Patachou in the Indianapolis International Airport, sipping a demi-tasse of espresso. The man called Hoppy was having plain old American coffee.

The elegant café was located in the airport's Civic Plaza, a spacious atrium with glass walls. *Better to hide in plain sight*, Kuzmich thought. Nobody would think of looking for him here.

Planes flew low over the glass ceiling, landing and taking off. Hoppy stared up at them, collecting his thoughts. He was running scared.

"What is so important that you insisted on seeing me?" said Kuzmich, barely hiding his anger. He didn't like being threatened with involving the FBI.

The words brought Hoppy's attention back to the man across the table. "I didn't sign on to be involved in a murder," he said, panic evident in his voice.

"You were well paid. And it is too late to undo what has been done."

Hoppy shook his head with disbelief. "When I read in the paper about that doctor dying of radiation poisoning, I knew it had to be your doing."

"What did you think I was going to do with that material
– power an atomic submarine?"

"I didn't know – I didn't think –"

"So what do you want to do about it? Turn yourself in?
Spend the rest of your miserable life in a Federal prison.
Partake of a lethal injection?"

"No, no. I'd never turn us in. You shouldn't think that."

The Azerbaijani frowned. "More money then. Is that
what this is about?"

"No, I just wanted to know what to do. Could you help
me disappear?"

Kuzmich thought to himself, *Yes, I will do exactly that.*
But he said, "Go home. Do nothing. Stick to your routine.
Everything will be fine."

"But a man is dead. The police –"

"The police can do nothing. Radiation poisoning is
difficult to trace. And if they do, the source is their own
nuclear facility." He smiled. "The nice thing is that there's a
lag between administering the dose and death. It gives one
time to get away. I was safely in California until you called
me back."

"But I –"

"You will not see me again. Do not try to contact me.
Our mutual friend will not know how to reach me, so don't
bother trying. Just go about your life and forget this. Enjoy
your money, but spend it carefully so as not to draw
attention to yourself."

"Why did you kill Dr. Kardashian? According to the
paper, he was well liked."

"This affair has nothing to do with you. You were just a
means to get the radioactive material." He was talking too

freely, but no matter. He had dumped the vial of liquid into Hoppy's strong black coffee while the man was staring up at the planes flying overhead. This problem would be solved in a day, maybe two. And he would be back in California by then.

"How did you know I could get my hands on radioactive material?"

"We got hold of a list of government contractors who worked on the Titan II silo project. You happened to be the first to take the $50,000. That's all."

CHAPTER NINETEEN

Weapons System

Being a journeyman pipefitter, Harry Casals had been hired to work on the US Air Force's LGM-25C Weapon System, a series of underground silos that housed 63 Titan II intercontinental ballistic missiles (ICBMs) with nuclear warheads aimed at the then-Soviet Union and China. The pay was good.

This Cold War program started up in 1963 and lasted until 1987 when the last Titan II was decommissioned. In the mid-70s Hoppy had helped build a silo about 100 miles northeast of Indianapolis.

The Titan II carried a W-53 warhead, the largest payload of any American ICBM. It had a yield of 9 megatons, the equivalent of 9-million tons of TNT. That's about 600 times more powerful than the bomb that destroyed Hiroshima. Capable of launching from its underground silo in just 58 seconds, it could deliver a nuclear warhead to a target more than 6,300 miles away within 30 minutes.

When the Titans were deactivated, most of them had been removed from their silos and stored at the Davis–Monthan Air Force Base in Tucson, Arizona, and Norton Air Force Base near San Bernardino, California. A few were overlooked. Later on, Titan II ICBM Site 571-7 has been converted into a museum displaying the actual Titan missile that still resided in that silo.

The site near Caruthers Corners was located on 40

acres of land at the end of Far Fields Road. A top-secret facility, it had been passed off as an automated weather observation station.

The Automated Surface Observing System (ASOS) was a joint effort of the National Weather Service (NWS), the Federal Aviation Administration (FAA), and the Department of Defense (DOD). It provided a handy cover story for hidden missile silos.

Hoppy knew the location of the maintenance entrances to the silo. Getting inside was a snap. The hardest part was cutting through the chain-link fence with his clunky wire cutters. At that time, there had been no guards at the abandoned facility.

Having been forgotten, the Titan stood 103 feet tall. Its warhead was still in place. Removing the cone, Hoppy cut into the core. The Titan II's warhead used enriched uranium for fission; a mixture of lithium and heavy hydrogen for fusion. He retrieved the pit containing the U-235 and returned to town to collect his $50,000.

~ ~ ~

The reported death of a prominent doctor by radiation poisoning set off several investigations. One by the Nuclear Regulatory Commission turned up records of a deserted ICBM silo in the area. A team was sent out to measure radiation levels to make sure there was no inadvertent residue from the nuclear warhead that had been stored there.

When investigators discovered that a fully functional Titan II missile was still in place inside the silo, that set off bells. They grew louder when it was found the warhead had been opened and fissile materials taken.

The US Air Force deployed a team of Special Ops to secure the facility.

These were the 'Men in Black" Police Chief Jim Purdue encountered.

CHAPTER TWENTY

Mosquito in the Sky

*T*he big black Sikorsky HH-60 Pave Hawk helicopter appeared on the horizon like an angry mosquito, its *whoop-whoop-whoop* sound assaulting the ears. Police Chief Jim Purdue and the movie star watched it land on a dusty cement helipad near a concrete building. As the blades slowed down, a two-star major general stepped down from the 'copter. A tall, stocky man with silvery hair, he wore an Air Force combat uniform. He carried his headgear under one arm, a briefcase under the other – a businessman warrior.

"Gentlemen," he said, "thank you for waiting."

Maj. Gen. Calvin LaRosa must have been bivouacked someplace close by, for the police chief and his passenger had only waited an hour for this arrival. Likely the 'copter came from Grissom Air Reserve Base, a joint-use facility located about 12 miles north of Kokomo. Maybe 70 miles away as the crow (or Sikorsky) flies.

"General, perhaps you can explain what's going on here? I'm not used to having my county invaded by the military."

That "my county" business was a bit of an exaggeration, in that the Caruthers Corners police department only had jurisdiction over the town, not the entire county. But now was not the time to clarify jurisdictions.

Gen. LaRosa looked unfazed, as if dealing with children

who had wandered from the safety of their schoolyard. "Chief Purdue, I've checked with HQ and Mr. Hitchinson's papers appear to be in order. He indeed bought this property last month at a government auction. Problem is, we have some left-behind equipment that needs to be removed before he can take possession. I hope you'll understand."

"What kind of equipment – some old weather vanes? Why would the Air Force be involved with an abandoned weather station?"

"What I'm about to tell you is classified. We will hold both of you liable if you repeat this. That National Weather Service malarkey was just a cover story. This is the site of a decommissioned ICBM silo that was once part of our nuclear deterrent fleet. When this LF was closed down in the late '80s, one of our birds got left behind."

Jim Purdue looked popeyed. "You mean to say there's still a nuclear missile here."

"I'm afraid so, but if you and Mr. Hitchinson will have a little patience, we'll dismantle it and have it removed within ninety days."

"What kind of missile is it?" asked Handsome Hitch, speaking for the first time. He'd once had a small part in a movie titled *Strategic Missile Command*. A straight-to-video production early in his career. But sales had been good.

"According to records, it's one of the Titan family. I haven't been down in the hole to look, but probably an LGM-25C."

"Hole? It's underground?" asked Chief Purdue.

"Yes," nodded the general. "This is a pretty standard

Launch Facility. That concrete building over there is the Missile Launch Control Center, usually manned by four technicians. And that tumbledown shack over yonder disguises the blast door at the top of the hole. Underneath it there's a vertical cylindrical hangar housing the bird. It could take out the Grand Palace in Kremlin Square in less than thirty minutes."

"And that bomb's been here in our backyard how long?"

"Since '76, according to my records."

"Holy cannoli."

"These anti-ballistic missile defense systems were designed to protect the US against incoming nukes from the Chinese or a limited Soviet attack."

"And the Air Force is responsible for this?"

"Only partly. Missile defense was originally the responsibility of the US Army. However, the Titan rocket family was established in October 1955, when the Air Force awarded a contract to the Glenn L. Martin Company to build us an ICBM. What is now the Missile Defense Agency took over responsibility for a layered defense against ballistic missiles in the early '80s."

"More than I want to know," said Chief Purdue. "Just get that thing outta here."

"Good. If I told you any more I'd have to shoot you."

"Very funny," said the police chief.

"I don't think he was kidding," said the movie star.

CHAPTER TWENTY-ONE

Home Again, Home Again

Maddy got to go home the next day. Orderly Joe Turner wheeled her out to the car. She could walk on her own now, but tired easily. At home a comfy daybed had been set up in the den, so she wouldn't have to worry about navigating the stairs right away.

The convoy from the hospital consisted of several vehicles: Mark with his brood in their Honda Odyssey, Freddie and his group in their Jeep, the Quilters Club in Lizzie's new Lexus, and Beau driving Maddy in that big Toyota Sequoia.

Earlier, Beau had picked up N'yen at the bus stop in front of Town Hall. Aggie was ecstatic to see her favorite cousin. The two were riding with their Grammy and Grampy, of course.

The gals had baked pies and cakes and strudel, throwing a Coming Home party of sorts. Maddy was fidgety, thinking she had been cooped up much too long. After all, the Quilters Club had patchwork quilts to complete for Watermelon Days ... and a murder to solve.

Two murders as it turned out.

Jim Purdue told everybody about the skeleton Wanda Schaeffer had found out near Never Ending Swamp. But he was careful to keep his mouth shut about the anti-ballistic missile facility at the end of Far Fields Road. That threat from Gen. LaRosa had sounded real.

Mark Tidemore edged close to the subject when he asked if Jim had been able to help his old college roommate.

Aggie perked up. "You mean Hitch Richardson. When can I meet him? I'm his greatest fan."

"Took him out to see the property," replied Jim. "He'll be able to take possession in a few months. The government has some equipment to clear out."

"Dad –!"

"Be patient, my dear. When Richie moves here we'll have him over for dinner," said her father.

"Well, okay."

"Are you talking about Hitch Richardson, the movie star?" N'yen spoke up. "I'm a bigger fan than you."

"Are not," said Aggie.

"Am too. I watched *Riders of the Lost Ark II* on TV the other night. That's my favorite."

Aggie nodded. "Didn't you love it when he saved the princess?"

"No, I liked it when he blew up the comet headed toward earth."

"Children, go play in the living room," suggested Tilly. They were all crowded into the den around Maddy's daybed. The living room was empty, except for Edgar Ridenour and Ben Bentley talking fishing. Let them deal with the kids. "Aggie, take your sisters and Donna with you too."

"Awww."

Maddy sat up in bed, feeling foolish to be lying there with everybody gathered around her like the viewing at a wake. "I'd like to call a meeting of the Quilters Club tomorrow," she announced. "Time to figure out these two murders."

"Sorry. I can't do it in the morning," said Lizzie. "I've promised to mend an Amish Wedding Quilt for Dan Sokolowski."

"We have quilts of our own to finish before Watermelon Days," Bootsie reminded them. "Perhaps we can bring our quilts over tomorrow afternoon and talk while we sew."

"Works for me," said Cookie. As secretary of the Historical Society, she made her own hours. The new exhibit wing wasn't officially open yet.

Okay," said Maddy. "Assemble!" Their code word for getting together, just like that quartet of Marvel Comics superheroes, The Avengers.

~ ~ ~

Hoppy wasn't feeling well. He seemed to have a slight fever. Was he catching the flu? He hated that tired, run-down feeling. Maybe he'd stop at Wal-Mart's Pharmacy for some Thera-Flu. That might help fight it off.

He parked near the entrance and nodded to the greeter as he entered the superstore. Heading down the aisle toward the 24-Hour Pharmacy, he passed the Hardware Department. There was ol' Darryl helping some guy pick out a power saw. Hoppy paused long enough to flip the salesclerk the bird. He'd found Mikhail without any help from that jerk, thank you very much.

There was a 2-for-1 sale on Thera-Flu, so his mood perked up. Maybe things were going his way after all.

~ ~ ~

Being in the neighborhood, Hoppy decided to stop by Sarge's Army-Navy Store. Located a few blocks from Wal-Mart, the small emporium sold more firearms than World War II backpacks or gas masks. The store's owner – Andy, there was no Sarge – said he needed another good war to help his inventory. But everybody knew he was just being a smart aleck. Iraq and Afghanistan kept him supplied with lots of surplus equipment.

Hoppy had been thinking about buying a gun. That business with Mikhail Kuzmich left him unsettled. Going home and forgetting about that doctor who had been poisoned with radioactive gloop wasn't going to work. Besides, he didn't trust the Azerbaijani. It might be a good idea to own a pistol, maybe a .380 mm Walther PPK like James Bond carries.

As he walked past the front counter, he heard a loud *click-click-click*. When he stepped closer to check out the sound, it turned into a clatter of clicks. *Cli-cli-cli-cli-clickety click*. "What the heck?" he said.

Andy turned in his direction. "That's an authentic 1960's era Civil Defense CDV 777 Radiation Detection Kit," he said. "A Geiger counter."

"Why's it making that sound?"

"I turned it on to demonstrate it for a customer. Guess I forgot to turn it off. Probably picking up the radium on your wristwatch."

"Radium?"

"Yeah, that's what makes your watch dial glow in the dark."

"But I'm not wearing a watch."

"Wow! The needle's all way over in the red zone. You're hot as a pistol. You sure you don't have a watch?"

CHAPTER TWENTY-TWO

A Rip in Time

L iz Ridenour showed up at the antique store promptly at 10 a.m. She brought along one of her sewing kits and a variety of threads. Matching the thread to the quilt fabric would be the biggest challenge in making an invisible mend.

Dan Sokolowski looked up when he heard the bell over the door. "Ah, thank you for coming," he said. "This is but a small repair. However, it would be a shame to leave a tear in this beautiful quilt." He nodded toward the off-white Amish Wedding Quilt that he had spread out on the big table.

Lizzie bent over the quilt to examine the breach in the fabric. "Hm, sharp edges. Looks more like its been cut, rather than torn."

"Can you fix it?"

"I think so. It won't be perfect, but it'll fool the human eye at first glance." She placed her sewing kit on the edge of the table and began comparing threads to the fabric. "Here's one that seems to match. This won't take long." *Piece of cake*, she thought. *I'll have time for coffee and pie at Cozy Café before I meet the girls at Maddy's house.*

The old man returned to his stool behind the counter, where he resumed examining the new jewelry under a bright light with a magnifying glass. He was looking for markings: initials, trademarks, designation of carats, whatever. The rings and necklaces from the Swisstown flea market were an exceptional find.

"What's this?" said Lizzie.

"What's what?' the old man looked up from the jewelry.

"Do you have a pair of tweezers?"

"Of course," he said, rummaging around in a drawer under the counter. He produced a pair, holding it up to show her.

Using the tweezers, Lizzie fished around inside the rent in the Wedding Quilt. "I felt something," she explained.

"Inside the quilt?"

"Here we are," she said. The tweezers extracted a slip of paper, folded in quarters, maybe measuring 2" x 3" overall.

The antiques dealer came around the counter for a closer look. "What is it, a note?"

"Seems to be." She unfolded the paper and read the handwritten message aloud:

> "*My husband intends to kill me.*
> *- Annabell*"

"This sounds like something we should report to the police," Lizzie said slowly, her green eyes as big as darning eggs.

"We may be a little late," replied Daniel Sokolowski. "This quilt is over a hundred-and-thirty-five years old."

~ ~ ~

Hitch Richardson was sitting in Mark the Shark's office. "This is going to make a great movie," he was saying. Handsome Hitch was wearing his West Coast Let's-Take-a-Meeting shades. "I've already talked to my agent. Caught him at Spago's last night. I'm going to commission Ken Lonergan to write the screenplay. We'll call it *The Lost*

Missile or *Inside the Forgotten Silo*. But in our version a terrorist discovers the ICBM and launches it toward Washington, DC. But our hero – that's me – saves the day. Whattaya think? A box office winner, right?"

"Hold on, Richie. Didn't you say Gen. LaRosa warned you and Jim to keep this to yourselves."

"No way, I'm doing that. This is much too big. It'll make a great summer blockbuster."

Mark Tidemore was too busy worrying about a nuclear warhead sitting ten miles outside of his town. Was there a health hazard? Could the warhead explode as the Special Ops tried to deactivate it? Would the publicity about it scare away new businesses?

"Here's one dollar," said Hitch, placing a greenback on the mayor's desk. "I want to option the movie rights from the town. A dollar should be binding for now, right? We'll work out a fair price later. For now, I want to claim the story."

Mark ignored the money. "Richie, I'm going to have to give the situation some thought. I need to talk with Chief Purdue and get his take on this."

"Don't take too long, Markie Baby. Snooze you lose. I might just buy the story rights from the Air Force instead."

"Good luck with that," said Mark the Shark.

~ ~ ~

Hoppy took to his bed. The Thera-Flu had done no good. He felt as if a freight train had run over him. *What if it wasn't the flu?* he thought in a moment of panic.

Hadn't that Geiger counter at the Army-Navy Store gone crazy? He was radioactive. Probably exposed himself when retrieving the pit from the Titan II's warhead. The uranium was supposed to be shielded inside a lead lining, but perhaps in the intervening years it had somehow leaked.

Was he suffering from radioactive poisoning? If so, he was probably a goner.

He remembered the story of a worker at United Nuclear in Rhode Island who accidentally put concentrated uranium solution into an agitation tank, exposing himself to 10,000 rad of radiation and died two days later.

Or what about Chernobyl, the USSR nuclear power plant disaster in 1986 where there were 29 fatalities from acute radiation syndrome. Most died within three weeks.

How long did he have?

CHAPTER TWENTY-THREE

A New Murder Victim

Jim Purdue looked at the unlikely pair across the desk from him – Lizzie Ridenour and Daniel Sokolowski. They had come to report a possible murder.

"Over a century ago?" the police chief rolled his eyes. "How do you expect me to investigate that? We don't know who this Annabell was or whether she was ever murdered."

"Thank you for your time, Chief Purdue," said the old man, getting to his feet. "We understand." It was obviously a lost cause.

Lizzie remained seated. "C'mon, Jim. Can't you do *some*thing?"

"Even if I found there had been a murder and was able to identify the killer, it would be for naught. The husband in question likely died more'n a hundred years ago himself."

She sighed, frustrated by the handcuffs of time. "Oh well, we tried. By the way, what have you found out about that skeleton Wanda Schaeffer found out at the Swamp?"

"Not much. I spoke with the FBI. No word of any Indianapolis mobsters gone missing. No Missing Persons reports that match."

This caught the old man's attention. "What do you know about the victim?"

"Male. Tall. Probably Caucasian. Blonde hair. We found a few strands among the leaves."

"How long has he been dead?"

"Doc Medford estimates about a month. The bones had been picked clean. Animals. The Swamp's full of 'em."

"But he died by gunshot?"

"Right. A bullet hole in back of his skull, execution style. That's why we checked on mobsters. But zilch so far."

"Somebody has got to be missing your bone guy," said Lizzie. "Everybody has somebody to notice their absence."

Chapter Twenty-Four
The List of Murders

The Quilters Club assembled in the Madison den, with Maddy holding court from her daybed. Bootsie, Cookie and Liz took the overstuffed chairs, while Aggie and N'yen sprawled on the plush carpet. Tilly had sent over her housekeeper to prepare watermelon tea and snacks. Mrs. Grottman was always happy to help out.

Everyone unpacked their partially finished quilts – except Lizzie who had finished hers – and organized their sewing paraphernalia. Fat squares and scraps of fabric covered the floor. N'yen was helping Aggie gather her Crazy Quilt pieces, as if he were her right-hand assistant.

Maddy looked much better than she had yesterday, maybe being home having something to do with it. "Ladies, we have two mysteries to solve," she called the meeting to order. There were no formal rules, but the women had fallen into expected patterns of behavior: Maddy leading them as they reasoned out criminal activities like a flock of latter-day Agatha Christies.

"What are these mysteries?" asked N'yen. Having arrived only yesterday, he was out of the loop.

"First up, we have the death of Dr. Kardashian," said Cookie. "Somebody fed him polonium-210."

"Then we have that skeleton Wanda Schaeffer found," enumerated Bootsie. "My husband needs some help with that one."

"And Daniel Sokolowski and I may have discovered

another murder," Lizzie added long-ago Annabell to the list, going on to describe finding the note inside the Wedding Quilt.

"Wow," said N'yen, "lots of murders to solve.

"Any connections between them?" asked Aggie, starting to sew on her Crazy Quilt's border. Under Lizzie's tutelage, she was close to finishing.

"Not likely," assessed her grandmother. "A radiation poisoning by the Russians, an execution by the mob, and an eerie note from 135 years ago."

"Okay, let's tackle them one at a time," suggested Cookie, always logical and orderly in her approach to things.

"Dr. K first," said Maddy. "Facts are these: He dropped dead in the hospital parking lot last week. Dr. K's death shows all the classic signs of Acute Radiation Syndrome. A toxicology screening showed traces of polonium-210. That was the radioactive element the Russians used to assassinate that dissident in London ten years ago."

"Did the doctor have any Russian connections?" asked Bootsie.

"None that we know of," said Lizzie.

"So why would the Russians kill him?" Cookie posed the question.

"We don't know that they did," Aggie said.

"But 95% of all the polonium-210 in the entire world is produced behind the Iron Curtain," replied Maddy, using the Cold War term for Russia. A sign of her Baby Boomer age.

"Could an ordinary citizen get his or her hands on polonium?" asked Aggie.

"Polonium is a very rare element in nature," Cookie

pointed out. "It's usually manufactured by irradiating bismuth with high-energy neutrons or protons. That takes equipment that only a government, a research facility, or a university has access to." She'd done her homework.

"Do tell," said Lizzie. Obviously unimpressed by her friend's detailed knowledge. She sometimes thought Cookie was showing off, like a teacher's pet.

"Are you sure it was polonium-210?" asked N'yen. "There are lots of other radioactive substances that could've killed him. Uranium-235, cobalt-60, iridium-192, you name it. Even X-rays and gamma rays and radon. Plutonium is considered to be the most toxic substance on earth."

"What about polonium?"

"It's right up there in toxicity."

"How do you know so much about this," challenged Lizzie, her head spinning with all these factoids.

"I read," he said with a shy smile.

~ ~ ~

Reaching no conclusion on the death of Dr. Kardashian, they moved on to the skeleton – the Bone Man they called him. Lizzie had been briefed on that case just this morning by Bootsie's husband. She reported, "The police think it's a mob hit, but they can't identify any likely victims."

"We don't have any mobsters around here," protested Cookie, having her finger on the town's pulse.

Lizzie shrugged. "They think it's some gangster from Indy whose body got dumped out of town."

"Never Ending Swamp would be a good place to dump a body," said Bootsie. "It might never have been found."

"Unless someone was walking her dog out there," added Aggie. A reference to Wanda Schaeffer and her

Chihuahua.

"What about DNA from the bones?" suggested Maddy.

"That's good if you have someone to match it to," said Bootsie. "So far Jim doesn't have a single prospect as to whom the dead guy might be."

"Why limit it to Indy?" asked Lizzie. "Aren't there lots of mobsters in Chicago and New York City?"

"Yes," said Maddy. "But they probably wouldn't transport a guy 200 miles to knock him off. New York would be even farther to travel."

"So it's a local crime?" said Lizzie.

"If you include Indy as local," said Cookie. "That's a little over 100 miles away. Would the mob take a guy that far to kill him?"

"Who knows what a mad-dog killer would do," exclaimed Lizzie, throwing up her hands in frustration. She knew nothing about mobsters and gangland executions.

"The Mafia are businessmen, not mad-dog killers," Maddy pointed out. "If they murder someone, it has a purpose."

"Well, if we can't identify the victim, maybe we should look for the motive," offered Aggie.

"It usually has to do with money," said N'yen. In addition to reading, he watched TV.

~ ~ ~

Then came Lizzie's turn to tell about the note she found inside Dan Sokolowski's quilt.

"This one should be simpler," said Cookie, the historian. "It was found inside an Amish Wedding Quilt that was made some 135 years ago. We know that by the quilt's design. And it came from the flea market at Swisstown, where there are fewer Amish than here. So all we need to do is find out if any new brides got murdered around 1880. We should be able to find that in back issues of the *Swisstown Bugle*. That little weekly has been going strong since 1862."

"I'll drive up with you tomorrow if you want to search back issues of the newspaper," offered Lizzie. She kind of considered this *her* case.

"Okay, you and I will tackle this one. Maybe Bootsie can keep us up to date on the skeleton case. And Maddy and Aggie can continue pushing on Dr. K's death."

"What about me?" said N'yen.

"You get to come with Grammy and me," replied Aggie. "You're my sidekick."

"How come I always have to be the sidekick," he complained. "You be the sidekick."

"It would be sexually insensitive to women's rights for a girl to be a sidekick," countered Aggie. "Besides, you've seen the movie *Despicable Me*. All Minions are yellow."

"Hey," said the Vietnamese boy, "that's an ethnic slur."

Aggie shrugged. "Don't talk to me. Take it up with the movie producers."

CHAPTER TWENTY-FIVE

Movie People

As it turned out, they did talk with a movie producer. That evening Hitch Richardson and a Hollywood filmmaker came by the Tidemore house to see Mark the Shark. Hitch was still dead-set on doing a movie based on the forgotten missile silo.

Elton J. Bakersfield had flown into Indy and drove down to meet Hitch in Caruthers Corners. He wanted to see this Titan II missile silo the movie star had purchased. It could save a ton of money to use a real silo as a setting for the movie. He already had a team of writers working on the script. Working title was now *Missile Attack from Below*, but that was still subject to change.

"My buddy's the mayor of this little town," Hitch was telling the producer. "He will see we get all the filming permits, whatever we need."

"Well –" began Mark.

"This production will bring plenty of money to the town," interrupted Bakersfield. "Accommodations, catering, rental fees for locations. And we'll use locals as extras."

"Extras?" said Aggie.

Bakersfield turned to the girl. "Be fun to be in a movie – right, honey?"

"Can I be a princess?"

"No princesses in this story. But I'm sure we can use you in a crowd scene."

"Me too?" asked N'yen.

"Maybe in the back. This story takes place in the Midwest. Americans only."

"I'm an American," the boy pointed out. "I was born in Chicago."

"Sure, sure, kid. That's great."

Hitch Richardson spoke up. "Mark, would the town be interested in putting up any money for the film? Better than investing in pension funds. And we could give you an Executive Producer title."

"We could find a role for you too," Bakersfield said to Tilly. "You're a real looker with that pale skin and blonde hair."

"Thank you," she responded. "I used to do some acting in high school." Her stage triumph had been second lead in the senior play, a production of *As You Like It*.

"I could see you had talent."

Mark replied to his ol' college roomie, "This is a small town, Richie. We don't have that kind of money to throw around. I'd get kicked out of office if I invested the town's meager funds in a long-shot movie deal."

"Nothing long-shot about this. I'm an A-lister now, highly bankable. I've got what *Variety* calls 'Marquee Power.'"

"I see all your movies," gushed Aggie. Obviously awestruck.

"Me too," said her cousin.

"Thanks, kids."

"I'm thirteen," she said, trying to make the point she was no longer a kid. Thirteen was the same age as Juliet in Shakespeare's famous play.

"That's a lovely time of life," Hitch smiled, "just budding into young womanhood."

"Yes, it is," she said, knowing that he understood. If he had a second-home in Caruthers Corners she'd get to see him on a regular basis. Romance might blossom. She could marry a movie star and still be close to her parents. But perhaps she was getting ahead of herself. She still had to finish high school.

"Did you really find a missile silo with a rocket in it?" persisted N'yen.

"You bet we did. Me and your Uncle Jim saw it. A hundred-foot-tall Titan II ICBM right there under the ground at that old weather station. Just like the Air Force left it back in the '80s ... except for some vandals trying to get into the nuclear warhead."

"There's a nuclear warhead?" Tilly's mouth dropped open.

"Did they take the plutonium or uranium?" asked N'yen, suddenly seeing a connection with the radioactive poisoning of Dr. K.

"Who knows?" shrugged Hitch. "You'd have to ask Gen. LaRosa. He's the man in charge."

CHAPTER TWENTY-SIX

Newspaper Archives

There was nothing Cookie liked better than thumbing through old newspapers. She considered that to be observing history firsthand. Real-time accounts of happenings in the past. The *Swisstown Bugle* stored nothing online or in a digital format. No microfilm or microfiche. Only a cavernous backroom, its shelves stacked high with yellowed newsprint stretching all way back to May of 1862, the week the *Bugle* printed its very first edition.

Cookie's position with Caruthers Corners Historical Society had been a door opener with the *Bugle*'s editor. News of its new wing was getting around.

"Oh my, where do we start?" said Lizzie, staring at the room filled with old newspapers.

"The problem with dating quilts is that we go by styles common to a period," explained Cookie. "But that doesn't account for outliers, quilts that look similar but were made at a different time. When Dan Sokolowski says circa 1880, it could range from 1870 to 1900."

"That's a thirty-year span," shrieked Lizzie. "Searching three decades of newspaper could take us days." She had a hair appointment tomorrow at Helen of Troy Spa and Beauty Salon that she didn't want to miss.

"Fortunately, it's a weekly newspaper, not a daily."

They started with 1880, working forward. If they found nothing there, they would work backward.

Much of the news was mundane. Barn raisings. Public meetings. A lost cow. A bank robbery. The death of a local citizen. Or the death of a celebrity, like English novelist George Eliot (Mary Anne Evans), who died on December 22, 1880, her 61st birthday.

They found a possibility early on, in the year 1883, the murder of Annabell Stoltzfus (née Yoder) by persons unknown. The new bride's body had been discovered by her husband Amos, a local cabinetmaker. She had been strangled with a rope.

"*Eureka!*" shouted Cookie.

"Thank goodness," muttered Lizzie. She had already broken a nail turning pages.

Thumbing through the month ahead yielded no follow-up story. Annabell Stoltzfus was dead and gone. Lost to history. Except for that singular notice.

At Cookie's insistence, they plowed on for another year and a half, until they found a wedding announcement, a union between one Amos Stoltzfus and Mary Wagler. It noted that he was a wealthy cabinetmaker, having come into a large inheritance a year or so ago.

From his first wife?

Continuing onward a few months, they found another obituary, this one for Mary. She had been strangled by persons unknown. It said she would be grieved by her loving husband. It mentioned that Mary came from Caruthers Corners, the daughter of Vernon and Lavinia Wagler.

"I think we may have a lady killer here," said Lizzie.

~ ~ ~

Chief Jim Purdue got a break in the skeleton case. One

of the Borkholder boys found a wallet over near Never Ending Swamp. Ten-year-old Atlee had been looking for lizards for his terrarium when he spotted a shiny leather object sticking out of the muck. This spot was maybe a half-mile from where Wanda Schaeffer found the femur bone.

Fishing the wallet out of the sticky mud, he took it home before opening it. Inside he found $520, all in twenties, a ticket stub for a Cineplex on the far side of Burpyville, a two-for-one coupon for chicken wings at the Mother Hen Café, a MasterCard in the name of Willard G. Manchester, and an Indiana driver's license made out to the same name. The license gave his address as a low-income apartment building in Burpyville.

An avaricious lad, Atlee pocketed $400 of the money, leaving enough in the wallet to seem plausible, then told his dad what he'd found. Leland Borkholder immediately drove his buggy down to Flynn's Texaco and asked Buddy Flynn to phone the Caruthers Corners police station.

"*Rief dr Polizei!*" he'd shouted until Buddy got him to calm down and speak English. Local Amish spoke a version of Swiss German, rather than Pennsylvania Dutch. The Swiss dialect has changed little in 200 years.

Chief Purdue arrived at the Borkholder farm within twenty minutes. He'd hit 80 MPH on that straight stretch past Flynn's Texaco, before turning onto State Road 102.

Leland and Sarah Borkholder lived in a white two-story farmhouse with their seven children. No wires ran to the house, for Amish eschew such "foreign technology" as electricity and phones and automobiles. The Borkholders used milking machines for their two-dozen dairy cattle, but the vacuums were powered by propane. Being a deacon of the church, Leland was careful to follow the *Ordnung*, a set of church rules that guided their austere daily living.

Deacon Borkholder was standing on the front porch, waiting for the police chief to arrive. He was wearing a solid-colored shirt, typical broadfall trousers with suspenders, and a straight-brimmed hat. Being married, he had a full beard but no moustache. He walked down the steep wooden steps to greet the policeman.

"*Grüezi,* he said. "Thank you for coming." Swiss German is spoken among the Amish family, but English is reserved for the outside world. As they like to say, *Ai Sprooch isch nie gnueg* ("One language isn't enough").

"How are you, Leland? Did you buy that horse from Boyd Aitkens?"

"*Yo*, she is a fine mare. I am using her for breeding."

"Your message said something about finding a wallet over near the Swamp."

"*Ich mues öppis mälde.* My son Atlee found this." He handed over the black leather wallet to the police chief.

"Can your boy show me the exact spot?"

Leland Borkholder gave a curt nod. "He will ride there with you." The farmer called over his shoulder, "Atlee, come!"

The boy appeared on the porch.

"Show *de polizischt* where you found the wallet. However, before you go, *gib ihm das gäld du gefunden hast.*"

The boy reluctantly handed over a wad of twenties. $400 – the money he'd hoped to pilfer. His father knew him all too well.

"*Du pfüderi, bisspöter. Bis spotter.*"

Borkholder gave an apologetic half-smile to Chief Purdue. "Atlee has yet to learn the virtues of honesty. My son will be a handful when he comes to the age of *Rumschpringe*. At that time he may choose not to follow our ways. A pity."

"I appreciate his help. I think this wallet may belong to a dead man we've been trying to identify."

"You speak of the bones *Frau* Schaeffer found over near the Swamp?" Word was out.

"That's right. I think there may be a connection."

"My son will show you where he found *dä portmone*. The boy is a *bensel*, but he will answer all your questions or face the paddle. Right, Atlee?"

"*Ja, papi.*"

~ ~ ~

Atlee Borkholder rode over to the eastern edge of the Swamp with the police chief. The boy wasn't used to being in an automobile and his brown eyes looked very excited.

Parking at the side of the road, they followed a narrow path along the edge of the boggy quagmire until they came to a large oak shaped like a V. Probably split by lightning, it marked the spot where the wallet belonging to Willard G. Manchester had been found.

Poking around with a stick, Chief Purdue was able to unearth a shoe and the chain for a pocket watch. A dumping ground for anything that might identify the dead man, he guessed.

CHAPTER TWENTY-SEVEN
The Summit

Maj. Gen. Calvin LaRosa had agreed to a meeting with Hitch Richardson and his producer. It was that or risk them going public with the story of a forgotten ICBM with a live nuclear warhead. Mark Tidemore had volunteered the Town Hall conference room as neutral ground. Hitch insisted his old roomie sit in on the meeting with them.

"You will have access to your property in sixty days," the general was saying. The Nuclear Regulatory Commission had given the deactivation a high priority, an attempt to "get rid of the evidence" before the movie star went to the papers.

Hitch's producer spoke up. "We wanted to talk with you about that, General. We'd like the missile to stay in place till after we finish shooting our movie."

"I'm afraid that is impossible," Gen. LaRosa shook his head. "It has been declared a potential health hazard."

That got the Mayor's attention. Anything that threatened the town was his concern. "Health hazard?"

"Potential, I said."

"My lawyer says that when I bought that property at auction, the price included everything on it. So one could argue that the missile belongs to me." Hitch smiled, having played his ace.

"National security trumps an auction," said the two-star general, looking toward one of the two officers he'd brought with him to the meeting. The lieutenant gave him a nearly imperceptible nod. Likely a JAG, the legal branch of the Air Force.

Hitch could feel his advantage slipping away. "What if we paid a million smackers to the Air Force for the movie rights and use of the missile for thirty days filming?"

The general chuckled but didn't dignify the proposal with an answer.

"There could be a juicy role for you in the picture too," added Bakersfield. The producer was holding back an Executive Producer credit as a bargaining chip, but that was coming next to sweeten the pot.

Gen. LaRosa snorted. "Me in a movie? What part would I play?"

"Yourself, of course. We want this to be accurate, just short of a documentary."

The general stood up, signaling that the meeting was over. "That's exactly what the Air Force doesn't want. If you try to make a movie about this incident – or go public with it in any way – you will be facing ten years in a Federal Prison. That falls under Title 18, Part I, Chapter 37, US Code § 798 - Disclosure of Classified Information, in case you want to look it up."

Hitch Richardson slumped back in his chair, defeated, as the general and his entourage marched out the door.

The general said, "Oh! Excuse me, madam," as he nearly bumped headlong into Maddy Madison and her grandchildren.

"Gen. LaRosa, you're just the man I want to see," she announced.

The general and his two officers seemed caught off-guard by this impromptu encounter. The civilian woman was blocking their passage. "And who are you?" he bellowed.

"That's my mother-in-law," interceded Mark Tidemore. "She was probably coming to see me. That's my daughter with her."

"No, we were looking for the general. Your friend Hitch told Aggie they were meeting here this morning."

"We have to go," the JAG officer tried to finesse their exit. "The general has a very tight schedule today."

"I'm sure he does," nodded Maddy. "However, I have one quick question. Does the nuclear warhead on your Titan II out on Far Fields Road contain any polonium-210?"

That caught the general off guard. "Of course not," he sputtered. "Polonium hasn't been used as an initiator in nuclear warheads since 1965. "

"So there was no polonium-210 in that warhead?"

"None. Now if you'll excuse me, madam." The general and his officers left the building.

~ ~ ~

Cookie knew the Wagler family, a quiet Amish clan who operated a big farm off State Road 102. Abram and Abigail Wagler were descendants of the Vernon and Lavinia mentioned in the *Swisstown Bugle*.

"*Yo*, Mary Stoltzfus was my great aunt," Abram confirmed. "She died young, shortly after marrying."

"Was there any hint of foul play?" brazenly asked Lizzie. That was her style, no filters.

"We do not speak ill of the dead," the man demurred.

His wife Sarah looked fidgety, then blurted, "There was always the family suspicion that Amos Stoltzfus murdered Abram's Aunt Mary for her dowry. But nothing could be proven."

"Sarah –" her husband cut her off. "It was so long ago."

"We think Amos Stoltzfus not only murdered your great aunt, but that he also killed his first wife, a woman named Annabell Yoder," Lizzie affirmed.

Abram shook his head slowly. "We know people named Yoder, but we've never heard of this Annabell ... or of Amos Stoltzfus having a wife before Aunt Mary."

"Do you know what happened to Amos Stoltzfus?" asked Cookie. Her own research had turned up nothing on him following that *Bugle* article.

"My mother told me he died around 1910 in a logging accident. But he was married so briefly to Aunt Mary we never accepted him into our family. Besides, he lived up in Swisstown. Nobody bothered to keep track of him."

A dead end. Lizzie was losing interest. "Well, thank you for your time."

"*Uf widerluege,*" he replied and turned toward his home, eager to get back to his chores.

Looking past him, Cookie could see about a dozen children peeking through the front windows. She knew Abram Wagler had a large family, a workforce for his farm.

"Are all of those your children?" Cookie said to Abigail Wagler.

"*Ja, füfzä.*"

"How many did you say?"

"Fifteen," she returned to English.

"And they work here on the farm?"

"All but the two eldest. Adam is employed at the E-Z Seat factory. Ephraim works as a carpenter."

"Where does your son do his carpentry work?"

"Ephraim is helping build a room onto a house in Burpyville, but the gentleman died and work has been suspended. A shame it is."

"A shame about losing the work?"

"Not that. We have plenty for Ephraim to do here on the farm."

"You mean about the man dying ..."

"*Ja*, that too. But I speak of his *frau*. Ephraim tells me she is *rutsching* with another man. It spites me to learn of this."

"You're saying the wife of the man who died was carrying on behind his back?"

She nodded her bonneted head. "*Ja*. My son witnesses the *schmunzla*. The man comes to *Frau* Kardashian's *haus* while the *dokter* works."

"That *is* shameful," Cookie agreed.

CHAPTER TWENTY-EIGHT

Amish in Indiana

*T*he Amish are traditionalist Christians who follow a simple, rural life. Located mainly in Pennsylvania and Indiana, they are direct descendants of Europe's early Anabaptist movement, the belief that baptism should be affirmed in order to be valid rather than bestowed on unknowing infants.

The Amish were a Swiss group that split off from the Alsatian Anabaptists in 1693, led by a semi-literate tailor named Jakob Ammann. Much of the disagreement was over the practice of shunning, the social ostracism of anyone who has been excommunicated from the church. Those who followed Ammann's strict disciplinarian approach became known as Amish.

In 1850, Old Order Amish settled in northeastern Indiana. Most were first-generation immigrants from Switzerland. Among themselves they continue to speak a form of Burmese German, while the Amish who settled in Pennsylvania speak a mainstream dialect of High German. When Amish people get together from other areas they have trouble understanding each other, so they inevitably revert to English.

In Indiana, Old Order Amish oversee 90 church districts in about 20 settlements. Worship services take place every other Sunday, alternating from home to home of members. While they all follow the guidelines of

Ordnung, each assembly is self governing, with its own set of rules determining the width of hat brims and whether buggies are covered or not.

Today, modern technology is used selectively by the Amish for fear it will weaken the family structure. Because 120-volt electricity connects to the outside world, it violates the Amish idea of separation from society. Automobiles are seen as a form of vanity. Telephones are thought to discourage face-to-face interaction. Television brings unbiblical values into the home.

Horses are used to pull wagons, buggies, and agricultural equipment. Engines are only allowed to run farm machinery and must be powered by propane or diesel generators rather than fixed-line grid electricity.

Anything that might be an intrusion on Amish values is avoided. The Amish may not travel on an airplane. Social Security or other commercial insurance is forbidden. Children attend school only through the eighth grade. Males are to wear hats when outside; females must keep their head covered, usually with a prayer bonnet.

Jewelry is never worn, not even wedding rings. Marital status is denoted by beards for men (but no mustache), and black bonnets for women. Unmarried boys must be clean-shaven. Amish are expected to marry other Amish.

Twice a year each church district holds a meeting led by its bishop to consider any changes to the *Ordnung*. If in the voting two or more people reject the proposed change, the guidelines remain unaltered. Tradition is maintained.

Today, more than a quarter-million Amish are found in the US and Canada. There are no Amish left in Europe.

~ ~ ~

Cookie found Ephraim Wagler repairing a roof at Wabash Acres, a new retirement development off Highway 21. He was a handsome young man, clearly a member of the Amish community based on his drab garb and suspenders instead of a belt to hold up his trousers. Still unmarried, his face was clean-shaven. She couldn't help but notice his eyes, as blue as Bennington marbles.

"*Grüezi, Frau* Bentley," he said as he climbed down the ladder. "*S'mueti* says I am to hear from you."

"Yes, I wanted to ask you about the man you saw with Dr. Kardashian's wife."

"*Wonnernaus*. That is not my business. I should not have told my mother."

"This is important. Dr. Kardashian is dead and this man may have been involved."

The boy ducked his head. "*Dä früünd isch es dokter wi de ehemann.*"

Having lived in Caruthers Corners all her life, Cookie had picked up a few Swiss German words. "You say her boyfriend is a doctor like her husband?"

"*Äbä*. That is right."

"Would you recognize this doctor –?"

Ephraim Wagler waved her question away. "I best go back to *das dach* ... the roof. It is going to make wet. I must work hurrieder."

Cookie glanced up at the sky. "Yes, it does look like rain," she nodded.

CHAPTER TWENTY-NINE
The Missing Orderly

The Burpyville Police confirmed that Willard Gilbert Manchester was missing. His neighbors had thought he was on vacation, but it turned out his car was in the garage and matching Samsonite was sitting empty in a closet.

Chief Frank Crenshaw identified Manchester as an orderly at Burpyville Memorial Hospital. He lived alone, had no known relatives, kept to himself. At the hospital someone had listed his absence as "on vacation." No one could identify the handwriting on the timesheet form.

By now, the FBI lab (at Chief Purdue's request) had examined the skull found at Never Ending Swamp and concluded it had been penetrated by either a 9mm or .360 fired at close range. Death was probably instantaneous.

Burpyville's police chief had sent follicles from Willard Manchester's hairbrush to the FBI for DNA testing. Everyone expected a match between the hair follicles and the deoxyribonucleic acid in the marrow of one of the bones found at the Swamp.

Having ruled it a homicide, Caruthers Corners Police Department and the Burpyville Police Department were going forward with a joint investigation.

Motive for the murder remained unknown.

~ ~ ~

Maddy called Nurse Natalie Thackeray and asked her what department of the hospital Willard Manchester worked in. Bootsie's husband wasn't being very forthcoming with information. He didn't want the Quilters Club – to use his words – "butting in."

"Hon, I work nights. I don't know this orderly you're talking about."

"But you could find out where he works, right?"

There came a silence over the phone. Then Nurse Thackeray sighed, "You're saying this Manchester guy might be dead?"

"The police seem to think so."

"Okay, I'll go ask. But I'm not sure what this has to do with your rehab program."

~ ~ ~

Hitch Richardson and Elton Bakersfield left town, heading back to Hollywood. The prospects for *Countdown to Death* (the latest working title) were dimming by the hour. Gen. LaRosa's threat of ten years imprisonment under Title 18 for Disclosure of Classified Information was daunting. The film was going into turnaround even before it got off the ground.

Hitch was rethinking his plans to build a getaway home in Caruthers Corners. He would talk with his real estate lawyer about getting out of the auction deal. Who wanted to live on top of a nuclear hellhole?

Bakersfield was already onto his next project, a super hero version of *The Wizard of Oz* – Dorothy, the Tin Man, the Scarecrow, and the Lion turned into an Avengers-like team due to planetary differences between Oz and Earth. He thought Hitch might be good for the Tim Man character, since Robert Downey Jr. was already committed to the Iron Man franchise.

Mark the Shark was demanding that the Nuclear Regulatory Commission provide the town with an Environmental Impact Report. Yesterday Mark and Chief Jim Purdue drove out to Far Fields Road to check out the abandoned silo, but their exploratory mission was thwarted when they encountered a team of men in HAZMAT suits swarming the property.

CHAPTER THIRTY

Pepper Upper

Nurse Thackeray reported back in about a half hour. "Willard worked in the Radiology Department," she rambled off the information. "That's on the basement level, just a few doors down from the Toxicology Lab. Dr. Horace Prepper is the hospital's Chief Radiologist."

"Do you think he would see me?"

"One step ahead of you. He said he's got an opening at 3 p.m. if you want to come by. I told him you were the mother-in-law of the mayor of Caruthers Corners."

"Thanks, Natalie."

"You sure you're up to coming. You're still recovering."

"No problem."

~ ~ ~

Maddy was feeling up to getting around, but wasn't ready to drive yet. So she prevailed on her daughter Tilly to ferry her over to Burpyville Memorial to meet with Dr. Prepper. Aggie and N'yen tagged along, of course. Mrs. Grottman watched the younger children.

"Yes, yes, I'm used to it," the doctor said as the women and kids crowded into his small office on the basement level of the hospital. "Most people call me Dr. Pepper. Or Pepper Upper."

Dr. Prepper looked far from being a "pepper upper." Ironically, he was a lethargic little man with drooping eyelids and no energy. His slow, deliberate movements reminded one of a sloth or a turtle.

Radiologists are specialist physicians who utilize a wide array of advanced techniques in medical imaging to diagnose and treat patients with all types of illness. These imaging modalities include X-rays, ultrasound, CT, and MRI examinations.

Certified by the American Board of Radiology, Horace Prepper had earned an MD from John Hopkins and completed a fellowship in Interventional Radiology at Yale. He was a good catch for a small hospital like Burpyville Memorial.

"Thank you for meeting with me," Maddy offered him her best smile. "As you may know, I was one of Dr. Kardashian's patients."

"Ah, yes, a tragedy about Elmer."

"I'm curious about how he may have gotten radiation poisoning."

"That's a puzzle."

"Do you have radioactive material in this department?"

"Indeed we do, but there's no chance Elmer Kardashian got exposed here. I don't think he ever set foot on this floor. He wasn't on the hospital staff, just had privileges."

"The curious thing is the toxicology report said he was exposed to polonium-210. But that's pretty rare, I'm told."

"Indeed it is. We certainly don't have any here. Never have. As far as I know, polonium's only manufactured in Russia."

"Is polonium easy to detect?"

"Quite the contrary. That's why the Russians use it as an assassination tool. But it can be identified if you look for it before it atrophies. Polonium is a radioactive element that exists in two metallic allotropes. The alpha form is the only known example of a simple cubic crystal structure in a single atom basis."

"And you can identify polonium as the cause of death?"

"Polonium-210 may be quantified in biological specimens by alpha particle spectrometry to confirm a diagnosis of poisoning in hospitalized patients or to provide evidence in a medicolegal death investigation."

"Could the toxicology report be wrong?"

"You mean Dr. Pettigrew made a mistake?" said Dr. Prepper. "That's not likely. He's a very meticulous man."

CHAPTER THIRTY-ONE

Agent in Place

Hopalong Cassidy staggered into the lobby of Burpyville Memorial and announced to the receptionist, "I think I'm dying."

"You've got the wrong entrance," she replied. "The Emergency Room is around to the side."

"Help me," he pleaded. "I-I'm about to collapse."

"We don't admit people at this desk. There are protocols to be followed. You'll have to fill out the proper forms, present your insurance or method of payment, give us the name of the admitting doctor, get assigned a room, things like that. Me – I just handle visitors."

"B-but ..."

"You look a little green around the gills. You really should go to the ER, let them take a look at you."

Hoppy took a deep breath. "A Russian has poisoned me," he began. "I'm radioactive. Probably glow in the dark. Can't you help me?"

"Radioactive?" Everybody in the hospital had been buzzing about Dr. Kardashian's death. The toxicology screening was now common knowledge. Death due to a lethal dose of polonium-210. The receptionist let out a loud scream.

But Hoppy didn't hear it. He had fainted onto the tile floor.

~ ~ ~

Bootsie wormed some information out of her husband. It took his favorite meal – prime ribs with watermelon sauce. No sooner than he sat down to dinner, he blurted all.

He told her that the FBI had scored a hit with the deoxyribozymes from the bones found at Never Ending Swamp. The VNTR (variable number tandem repeat) loci had matched up with one Viktor Ivanovich Medvedev. A Russian intelligence agent, Medvedev was known to be a lieutenant in the *Glavnoye razvedyvatel'noye upravleniye*, or the GRU as it's commonly called. He had dropped from sight several years ago. Now the FBI knew where to find him – at the Burpyville City Morgue.

DNA profiling is a forensic technique used to identify individuals by a small set of DNA variations, as unique as fingerprints. With over 10-million records, America's Combined DNA Index System (CODIS) is the largest such database in the world.

Turns out, the hair follicles of Willard Gilbert Manchester were also a hit. Manchester and Medvedev were in fact the same man. Apparently, the people-shy orderly was what's called an "Agent in Place" – an undercover spy.

What was a Russian spy doing in Indiana?

And who killed him?

~ ~ ~

Mikhail Dmitriyevich Kuzmich was now working at a Home Depot in Burbank, California. His references from the Hardware Department of that Wal-Mart in Indiana had got him hired. Russian Agents in Place either went high or low. Infiltrating the US government at its highest levels, or taking menial jobs that didn't draw attention to them.

Kuzmich was a low-level guy.

He and Viktor Medvedev had been sent to Indiana to recover the uranium from an abandoned ICBM in a silo near a town called Caruthers Corners. Locating it had been – what was that term Americans used? – "like finding a needle in a haystack." They had no luck until they turned up that pipefitter who had helped build the silo.

Then Viktor got greedy, selling some of the U-238 to a man who wanted to get rid of his girlfriend's husband. A stupid move. The death by radiation poisoning had drawn the attention of The Nuclear Regulatory Commission. Now men in HAZMAT suits were crawling all over that Titan II silo. Obviously, the Air Force was now aware that the radioactive pit of their nuclear warhead was missing.

Mikhail's controller had ordered him to sever all links that could lead back to Mother Russia, so Viktor had to go. As did that pipefitter. Now there was no connection other than himself. He worried that his controller might see fit to eliminate him too. He had two options: Take his chances with his higher ups, or defect to the US.

He thought about these choices as he waited on a blue-haired lady who wanted to buy a hammer.

CHAPTER THIRTY-TWO

Coffee Klatch

The Quilters Club met for coffee at Cozy Café that next day. They crowded into the big corner booth that would hold five – six with a chair on the end. After Maisie poured them cups of Maxwell House (and mixed chocolate milks for Aggie and N'yen), the waitress treated everybody to slices of just-out-of-the-oven watermelon pie. After all, they were good customers.

Maddy summarized the findings. "We have three separate murders. Dr. K the victim of radiation poisoning. A hospital orderly shot in the head. And a couple of brides likely strangled by their husband in the 1880s."

"They may not be all that separate," Cookie pointed out. "When Lizzie and I talked with the great-nephew of Mary Stoltzfus, we learned that Dr. K's wife might be having an affair."

"Do tell," said Bootsie. "With whom?"

"We don't know. But Abigail Wagler's son Ephraim saw them together when he was adding a room to Dr. K's house. He said they were *rutsching*. I looked it up. It means 'squirming' or 'fooling around.'"

"Hard to believe Veronica Kardashian's having an affair," said Lizzie. "She certainly played the grieving widow when I dropped by to see her with those flowers. Do you think she might be involved in her husband's death?"

"The husband or wife is always the first suspect," said

Bootsie. She'd learned that from her cop-hubby.

"Where would she get polonium?" frowned Lizzie. "They don't stock it at Helen of Troy."

"From the warhead on that Titan II ICBM out at Far Fields," suggested Cookie.

"No," Maddy shook her head. "Gen. LaRosa said that warhead didn't contain any polonium."

"And you believe him?" said Lizzie."

"Kinda."

"Doesn't matter whether it had any or not," interjected N'yen. "Polonium has a half life of 138 days. That means in about four-and-a-half months it turns to lead due to alpha particle emission. That Titan II has been down there since the '70s, so even if it did contain any polonium there wouldn't be any left by now."

"Wow," said Cookie. "How did this boy get so smart?"

"I read," he shrugged.

Maddy pushed on. "Okay, if Veronica didn't get polonium to poison her hubby from the warhead, where did it come from?"

"It's only made in Russia," Cookie pointed out. "Wasn't your original theory that the Russians did it ... like with that dissident in London?"

Lizzie frowned. "But we don't have a Russian connection."

"Sure we do," said Bootsie. That's when she told them about Viktor Ivanovich Medvedev, a match to his DNA turned up by the CODIS database.

"Double wow!" said Cookie. "This is turning into a John le Carré novel."

"Who?" said Lizzie. The redhead wasn't a book person,

sticking to her "stories" on TV.

"A British writer whose real name is David Cornwell," explained Cookie. "He writes spy stories. He worked for MI6 before taking up the pen."

"MI6 stands for Military Intelligence, Section 6," added N'yen. "That's Great Britain's Secret Intelligence Service." Reminding them that he read a lot of books.

"There's another Russian connection," said Maddy. "A guy named Harry Casals checked into Burpyville Memorial yesterday with symptoms of Acute Radiation Syndrome." Nurse Thackeray had called her this morning as soon as she got off her shift at the hospital.

"I hadn't heard about that," pouted Bootsie. Her husband failed to mention that piece of information. Maybe he hadn't got the news yet.

"Casals was babbling about a Russian slipping him a U-238 cocktail," continued Maddy.

"That's uranium, not polonium," Cookie pointed out.

Aggie wrinkled her brow. "How do we know Dr. K got a dose of polonium instead of uranium?"

"The toxicology report said polonium," Maddy reminded her.

"What if the toxicology report was wrong?" said the girl. "Maybe the lab made a mistake."

Maddy shook her head. "That's not likely. According to one of his colleagues, Dr. Felix Pettigrew doesn't make mistakes."

"But polonium's hard to detect," N'yen said. He was becoming quite the nuclear expert. He was sitting there with his iPhone, Googling as they talked. "It's surprising he found it in the first place. You almost have to be looking for it, it says on Wikipedia."

"You can't trust information on Wikipedia," Aggie said.

"Can too."

"Cannot."

"Children," Maddy hushed them. "We have a murder to solve."

"Four murders," corrected Bootsie. "Soon to be five if that guy Harry Casals dies."

"Who?" Lizzie was having trouble keeping it all straight.

"The plumber who turned up with radiation poisoning last night," Maddy reminded her.

"We should talk with him," said Cookie. Needing more facts to process.

"He's radioactive," Lizzie observed. "Won't it be dangerous to get near him?"

"It's not catching, like chicken pox," said Bootsie.

"People who are internally contaminated can expose people near them to radiation from the radioactive material inside their bodies," N'yen reported after a quick search on his iPhone.

"But you have to come in contact with the person's bodily fluids like blood, sweat, or urine," added Aggie, looking over her cousin's shoulder.

"Simple," said Maddy. "We just don't let Harry Casals pee on us."

~ ~ ~

After much discussion it was decided Bootsie would call on the radioactive plumber. No need to risk everybody. Maddy was still weak from her stroke, Lizzie too uninterested, and Cookie had details about the opening of the Historical Society's new wing to attend to. And nobody was going to let the kids go.

Besides, Bootsie could likely get in to see the man, being wife of the police chief.

It was easier than they expected. She bumped into the Burpyville police chief in the hospital lobby. She'd dated Frank Crenshaw in high school before hooking up with Jim in her senior year. He'd long been married to Bitsy Yost, sister of the woman who owned Helen of Troy Spa and Beauty Salon, but he still seemed happy to see Bootsie. As she recalled, he'd always had a thing for plump women; his wife was quite a porker too.

"Bootsie Purdue, what are you doing here? I just got off the phone with your husband five minutes ago."

"Hi, Frankie. I wanted to talk with that guy who came in last night with radiation poisoning."

"Uh-oh, sounds like you and your quilting buddies are sticking your nose into this case. Jim ain't gonna be happy about that."

"And you?"

"Heck, I can use all the help I can get."

"So I can see this Harry Casals guy?"

"Sure, go on up to the ICU. Tell my deputy I said it was okay."

CHAPTER THIRTY-THREE

The Dying Man

Hoppy Casals was not looking good. His hair was starting to fall out by the clumps, like a patient in an advanced stage of chemotherapy. His skin was waxy and gray. A glazed expression on his face, he was barely conscious.

The absorbed dose of radiation is measured in a unit called a gray (Gy). Diagnostic tests that use radiation, such as an X-ray, result in a small dose focused on specific organs — typically well below 0.1 Gy.

Symptoms of radiation sickness usually don't appear until the entire body has absorbed a dose of at least 1 Gy. Doses higher than 10 Gy are not treatable and typically lead to death within two days to two weeks, depending on the dose and duration of the exposure.

Dr. Madhuk Kapoor estimated that Casals had ingested about 8 Gy of radiation. The toxicology report said it came from a low-grade uranium.

"Not polonium?" queried Bootsie. "That's what killed Dr. K."

"There must be two separate sources," shrugged Dr. Kapoor. "Perhaps the incidences are not related."

"How many case of radiation sickness has this hospital had in the past ten years?"

"None, I would venture to say. It is not a common thing."

"Exactly," she said, like Perry Mason excusing a witness.

Bootsie was staring at Hoppy Casals through the glass wall of the ICU. "Am I in any danger being this close to him?" she whispered to the Indian doctor.

"No, most of his sickness is internal. At this distance with no physical contact you should be safe. You'd get more radiation sitting close to your TV set."

"Oh my. I may quit watching 'Cops.'"

"You said you had some questions for Mr. Casals ..."

"Yes. Can he hear me?"

"He will be able to hear you when I switch on this intercom. Are you ready?"

Bootsie nodded.

Klick.

"Mr. Casals, my name is Bootsie Purdue. I'm the wife of Police Chief Jim Purdue over in Caruthers Corners. He's working with Chief Crenshaw on your case. May I ask you a few questions?" So she stretched the truth a little. Jim and Frank *were* working together on that other murder, weren't they?

Hoppy's eyes opened slowly, like a lizard coming awake. "I already told Crenshaw everything I know. The Russian. Breaking into the missile silo. The fifty grand. Don't look like I'm gonna get to spend it now. I'm done for."

"Tell me about the Russian, if you don't mind repeating it."

"Mikhail Kuzmich, but I knew him as Michael."

Bootsie leaned closer to the glass. "You think he poisoned you with radioactive material?"

"Uranium that I took from the warhead of that Titan II. Either I got contaminated while removing it, or that Russkie slipped me a mickey."

"Why would this Mikhail do something like that?"

"To shut me up. I'm the only connection between the Russians and the stolen fissile material. When I'm gone, there'll be no way to trace it back to the Reds."

"What do they want with the uranium?" she asked. "Don't they have plenty of their own?"

"Probably. But it's hard to smuggle into the US. Maybe they want to build a bomb here."

That was a scary thought. But the plump lady with the short pixie haircut plowed on. "Where is this Mikhail?"

"Dunno. California, I think. He skipped town." Hoppy seemed to drift off for a moment, then snapped back. "What were we taking about?"

"Did you know Dr. Elmer Kardashian?"

"He's the doc who died of radiation poisoning … like I'm doing?"

"Yes. Could this Mikhail have been involved in that?"

"Michael all but admitted it. But I have no idea why."

"You said he paid you $50,000 to steal the uranium?"

"Yeah, a lot of good that will do me now. You want it?"

"How did you know how to find the uranium for Mikhail?"

Hoppy seemed to doze off, then opened his eyes and said, "What?"

She repeated her question.

"Oh that. I was one of the contractors who helped build the silo for the Air Force. So I knew the layout pretty good."

"Could you identify this Mikhail in a lineup?"

"Sure, if I last that long. But he used to work at Wal-Mart. They've probably got a picture of him in their personnel files."

~ ~ ~

Since she was already in the neighborhood, Bootsie drove over to Wal-Mart and asked to see the personnel manager. She was surprised when a clerk directed her to Fat Karl Schaeffer's office.

"Karl, what are you doing here?" she blurted. "Last I heard, you were keeping books for Aitkens Produce."

"Hello, Bootsie. I've been working here at Wal-Mart for the past two years. What brings you down to Burpyville?"

"Oh, I'm running an errand for my husband," she fibbed.

"How is the Chief?"

"Busy. He and Frank Crenshaw are working together on a couple of cases."

"Bet you Quilters Club ladies crack 'em first. I follow your adventures in the *Gazette*."

"Why thank you, Karl."

He leaned back on his bench, ready to do business. "Tell me, what can I do for you today?"

"My husband wants me to pick up a picture of one of your former employees, a man named Mikhail Kuzmich. I assume you've got a photo in your personnel files."

"You too?"

"Me too what?"

"A week or so ago, some nutcase came in here looking for Mikhail. But he quit a good month ago."

"Do you remember the name of this nutcase?"

"Didn't say. A short guy with wild hair."

"Sounds like Harry Casals. Some folks call him Hoppy. Used to have a plumbing business over in Caruthers Corners."

"Hoppy's Plumbing & Refrigeration? I've seen the truck. Didn't recognize 'im."

"I just visited him in the hospital."

"What's he got – the flu?"

"Something like that."

"I've heard a summer flu's going 'round."

"About that picture –?"

"Did you bring a warrant?"

Bootsie frowned. "Warrant? Why would I need that?

"You know I can't release personnel info without being compelled to do so. It's the law. But Jim knows that."

"Yes, but I just happened to be over here in Burpyville and thought I'd save my husband a trip. Can't you just give me the picture and we'll catch up on the paperwork later?"

"Can't do that. I'd get in trouble with my boss."

"It couldn't hurt to let me peek at Mikhail Kuzmich's photo. That way I'll have a better idea what the warrant is for."

Fat Karl looked conflicted. "I oughta check with my boss."

"C'mon, Karl. I have to get home and fix dinner."

Dinner resonated with him. He wife was cooking pot roast tonight. "Well, okay. But don't tell nobody I did this." He clicked a few keys at his computer and said, "Here you go."

Bootsie leaned over his shoulder to stare at the computer screen. The headshot of Mikhail Kuzmich was blurry, but she could make out the features: Thin face, close-set eyes, heavy brows.

The police chief's wife couldn't place it, but she had seen this man somewhere before.

~ ~ ~

About a month ago Bootsie had been coming out of the Family Dollar Store, arms laden with plastic shopping bags.

She bought all her cleaning supplies here, the prices being cheaper than at the Food Lion, and the Family Dollar was a lot closer than Wal-Mart down in Burpyville.

She hoped nobody spotted her with all these plastic bags, for she and her gal pals had vowed to use only paper to help protect the environment. Global warming and all that ... although she wasn't sure how plastic bags affected the earth's temperature.

She'd parked her car in front of the police station so she wouldn't have to feed a meter. Patty Pringle, the town's part-time meter maid, was ruthless in her ticketing, but the little Hun didn't dare touch Bootsie's new Jeep Cherokee when it was parked in front of the police station.

As she slogged past Cozy Café on her way to her car she nearly bumped into two men coming out of the diner's revolving doors. "Oops," she gasped, juggling the plastic bags to keep from dropping them.

"Here, let me help you," said a tall man with blonde hair. He helped her steady the armful of bags.

"*Chërt voz'mí!*" growled the other man, wrinkling his heavy brow. "Let her manage her own parcels."

"*Vsë puchkóm,*" replied the first man, making sure she had a good grip on her bags of cleaning supplies before stepping back.

"*Ty menjá dostál!*" continued the second guy. "You have endangered the project. You took *zélen'* for *ypaha bocca*."

"*Rasskazhí éto komú-nibúd' drugómu.*"

"You will care when you wind up as a *zhmúrik! Délo drjan'.*"

"I needed the money. I will give you half if you promise to shut up."

"*Ty che o'khuel blya? Bocc ub'yet nas oboikh.*"

"*Pyeryestan' zalupatsa.* The boss won't know about this if you just keep your mouth shut."

"*Ti durak,*" said the one with a mole on his cheek.

Bootsie walked on to her Cherokee and piled the Family Dollar bags in the backseat. "Foreigners," she huffed. "How rude."

She had not given the two men another thought.

CHAPTER THIRTY-FOUR

Maddy's Recovery

Maddy was doing her exercises. Among those who experience a stroke, 40 percent have moderate to severe impairments that require special care. She had been on the lucky side of that equation. Today she was doing arm and hand exercises that involved stretches. Next would come the motion exercises that prevented spasticity and improved mobility around joints.

She was thinking about signing up for a yoga or tai chi class. They had them over at the Hoosier Senior Recreational Center. Tilly took yoga there last year.

An hour or so earlier, Nurse Thackeray had phoned to tell her that Harry Casals passed away during the night. His heart failed; the official time of death was 3:21 a.m. As night nurse, she had been at his bedside. His last words were, "Why did I ever trust a Russian?"

Maddy considered his words. Was it a confession? Recrimination? Rhetorical statement? Or simply an ironic comment?

While doing her arm exercises she thought over the connections between the murders. Dr. K had been killed by a method used by Russian agents. The bones from Never Ending Swamp belonged to a Russian agent. And that plumber said he'd been poisoned by a Russian agent who had hired him to steal uranium.

What was the common denominator?

Russians.

~ ~ ~

Aggie and her cousin were sitting at the kitchen table with their Grammy. Peanut butter and watermelon jelly sandwiches were on the menu for lunch. Topped off with a tall glass of milk.

As they ate, Maddy talked them through her reasoning about the Russians. A way of double-checking her logic. She wasn't sure whether or not there were any mental after-effects of the stroke that might cloud her reasoning. Explaining it out loud made the facts seem clearer in her mind.

"That ties them all together," she concluded.

"Maybe, maybe not," said N'yen, sipping his milk. Wishing it had chocolate syrup in it. He liked the Hershey kind that came in a squirt bottle. That way he could adjust the chocolaty flavor to his taste.

His grandmother furrowed her brow. "What do you mean?" she asked the boy.

"Why not look at it from another angle?" he said.

"What other angle?"

"From the murder weapon angle."

She leaned forward so as not to miss a word. "How so?"

N'yen finished off his glass of milk. "There's no common – what do they call it on cop TV shows? – *modus operandi*, no connection between the types of murder weapons. Your doctor friend got injected with polonium-210. That plumber guy drank a solution of uranium-235. The Bones Man got shot in the head. And those long-ago Amish women were strangled. All different."

"Two of them were by radioactive poisoning," she

argued. "That's a commonality."

N'yen shrugged. "Polonium and uranium are different forms of radioactive material. And Gen. LaRosa said there was no polonium in that Titan's warhead."

"That's the confusing part," Maddy said. "Where did the polonium come from?"

"It had to come from the Russians," argued Aggie. "That's the only country where it's made. Isn't that what that Dr. Fitzwilliam down in Bloomington told you?"

"Yes. And Dr. Kapoor said the same thing."

"But what I can't figure out," said Aggie, "is if the Russians had polonium to use on Dr. K, why would they need to break into that warhead for uranium?"

"Maybe there's no connection between the two crimes," N'yen repeated.

"But both involved Russians and a radioactive material," said Maddy. "Don't you think that's a little too much of a coincidence?"

~ ~ ~

Apparently the FBI agreed. Special Agent Neil Wannamaker phoned Police Chief Jim Purdue to inform him the Feds had located Mikhail Dmitriyevich Kuzmich in Burbank, California, but he had given them the slip. A 28-man SWAT team surrounded the Home Depot where he worked, but Mikhail Kuzmich had not shown up that day. Somebody had tipped him off.

"You boys got a leak," said the police chief.

"Do not."

"Do too," he said, sounding like a conversation between Aggie and N'yen.

"The Feebies have connected the dots," Jim Purdue

reported that afternoon. He and Bootsie were hosting a cookout – all their close friends invited. "This Kuzmich character and his fellow spy Viktor Whatshisname hired Harry Casals to break into the missile silo and steal the uranium. Must have been a falling out between thieves, because Kuzmich shot Viktor. The FBI also thinks Kuzmich killed Dr. Kardashian and Casals – Casals because he was a link to get rid of, Kardashian they haven't figured out yet."

Beau said, "Looks like that about wraps it up. You and Frank Crenshaw can close out your cases; our wives can go back to quilting."

"Now if the Air Force will get that big missile out of our backyard," said Mark the Shark, "the town can get back to normal."

"A nuclear missile ten miles away," sighed Ben Bentley. "Who woulda thought?"

"Russian spies," said Edgar Ridenour, "that's hard to believe."

"No place is safe," sighed Beau Madison.

CHAPTER THIRTY-FIVE

Another Stolen Car

Deputy Hitzer got a call from the dispatcher. Another stolen car, Billy Ray Purdue's canary-yellow Lamborghini. That shouldn't be hard to spot, he thought.

And sure enough it wasn't. The minute he clicked off the radio, a blur of yellow whizzed past him on Old Farm Road. Wow! That 'ghini musta been doing 90. He flipped on his overheads and siren and gave pursuit.

He never would have caught it if the low-slung Italian sports car hadn't spun out on the curve. Fortunately, the $399,500 automobile wasn't damaged, other than losing a little tread on the 335/30 ZR 18 Pirellis. The tire marks stretched a quarter mile on the asphalt.

Sitting behind the wheel was that snot-nose juvie, Johnny Bristol. His father was a judge, so he usually got cut loose with a warning.

Not this time. "You're under arrest for grand theft auto," said the deputy. "Step out of the car please."

"Aw, c'mon, Petie. I didn't steal this bolt of lightning. I was just going for a joyride. No harm, no foul."

"Step out, Johnny. This is not the first time I've caught you in a car you didn't own."

"You're just wasting your time, bro. Daddy will make a phone call."

~ ~ ~

Aggie just couldn't pull it off: A double tumble. Her

gymnastics teacher was a total ogre. She'd practiced and practiced and practiced, but she still couldn't do it smoothly. She landed on her knee, on her elbow, on her butt. Not on her feet. She was sure to get a failing grade.

No, Aggie wasn't happy about summer school. After all, she was on the honor roll. Why should she have to go through such humiliation?

The principal had given her this second chance at passing phys ed. If she did so, her honor roll status would remain intact. PE was either Pass or Fail.

However, Aggie had never been a very athletic girl. She wasn't any good at volleyball. Stunk at basketball. Showed little promise at bowling. Even flopped at Ping-Pong. How could they expect her to pass tumbling?

Walking home, she circled through the town square. As expected, her cousin N'yen was waiting for her at the bandstand. He liked to sit there and watch the koi swim about in the Jacob Caruthers Memory Pond. Despite being her best-est friend in the whole wide world, he was definitely a weirdo. "Hi, N'yen," she waved her greeting.

He waved back and stood. "You're late," he noted.

"Almost sprung my ankle. I had to go see the school nurse."

"There's a nurse during summer school?"

"Only on Tuesdays. And this is –"

"– Tuesday," he concluded.

"You're so smart."

"Thank you," he said, missing her sarcasm.

"What do you think of my Russian theory about the murders?"

"You mean our Grammy's theory …?"

"We share the same conclusion," she clarified.

"There are Russians involved, that's f'sure. But I'm not so certain they killed Dr. K."

"But he's the one who was poisoned by that polonium that only comes from Russia."

"Yes, that's the strange part I can't figure out. The toxicology report couldn't be wrong about a key point like that, could it?"

~ ~ ~

Daniel Sokolowski was there when Tom the deliveryman and his halfwit brother dropped off another load of antiques. Sokolowski had scored big at the Swisstown flea market this week. An extra trip.

He checked off the inventory as they unloaded it: an early 1900s Hoosier kitchen cabinet, a 1940s burled walnut dresser and mirror, a Jacobean carved oak dining room buffet, a Robert W. Irwin hand-painted chest of drawers, a 1920s Federal Hepplewhite double pedestal dining table, an early-1900s Kochs cast-iron barbers pole, a stateroom steamer trunk with antiqued French finish, a vintage Tuscan wine corking machine, an 8 ¼"-high Pompeian bronze horse, a 1930s 14" x 11" WPA silkscreen Red Devil fire poster, a late-1800s Irish 2-piece crochet lace wedding gown, and a 1905 Elgin 15-jewel silver pocket watch.

While Tom was there, he asked him if he knew anyone named Stoltzfus up in Swisstown. Tom seemed to recall an old man by that name on the north side of town. "Amos, I think his name is," the deliveryman said.

"Thanks, that's the one I'm looking for. Must be a grandson."

"He's almost a hermit. Never goes out," Tom added. "He was shunned years ago and left the Amish church."

"Old Order, huh?"

"Old as they get."

CHAPTER THIRTY-SIX

Preparing for the Festival

Watermelon Days was coming up soon. Kicking off on Sunday with its big parade, everybody in Caruthers Corners skittered about with last-minute preparations. Mark Tidemore was meeting with the Watermelon Days Committee to tie up any loose ends. This year it was chaired by Hilda Hoople, last surviving member of the Hoople Quadruplets. Once a semi-recluse, her philanthropic work had brought her out of her shell. She had donated $20,000 toward promoting the festival. They were expecting up to 50,000 visitors this year.

These would mostly be day-visitors, since there was only one small motel in town, good for 30 people max. But people would be driving in from Indy and Burpyville and Fort Wayne, like an influx of lemmings.

Not to be outdone by Hilda Hoople, Bobby Ray Purdue had coughed up an equal amount to buy a used Ferris wheel from a traveling carnival that would become a permanent addition to the town square. Kind of like the Eye in London, but this one was creaky and slow. An ancient Atro Wheel built in 1967 by Chance Rides, it offered 16 gondolas that held 2 passengers each.

Freddie Madison was polishing up the big Kohler fire engine. Ben Bentley and Big Bill Haney were readying the animals from the petting zoo. Bobby Ray Purdue was organizing the volunteer clowns. The Polk sisters were baking watermelon pies along with all the members of the Women's Club. The Caruthers High band was practicing its John Philip Sousa medley. And vendors were readying the booths they would erect along Main Street.

It was rumored Boyd Aitkens had a watermelon that would top last year's 312-pounder. And Fat Karl Schaeffer was looking forward to the Watermelon Eating Contest.

A tractor-pulling competition had been added at the last minute. Errol Baumgartner claimed to have the lock on that, having bought a new John Deere 9620R for his farm. With 620 horsepower, this four-wheel-drive tractor was the largest John Deere ever built.

The Quilters Club gals were readying their entries in the quilting contest. Three-time state champion Holly Eberhard would be the one to beat. Lizzie had a shot with her innovative new take on the Jacob's Ladder motif.

The Jacob's Ladder pattern has been called many names: Stepping Stones, Underground Railroad, Road to California, Off to San Francisco, Gone to Chicago, and Trail of the Covered Wagon. All speak of going somewhere.

In the first known book on quilting (1915) Marie Webster wrote: "The bold and rather heavy design known as 'Jacobs Ladder' is a good example of a pieced quilt."

Described as a Bible quilt, its stepping stones design references a quote from Genesis 28:11-22: "*And he dreamed and behold a ladder set up on the earth and the top of it reached the heavens and behold the angels of God were ascending and descending on it.*"

However, Lizzie gave it a little twist, adding bright yellow angelic bows to a rather straightforward blue-and-white block pattern design.

Meanwhile, Cookie was putting finishing touches on her Amish Sunshine and Shadow Quilt. Bootsie was bumbling about with a Baltimore Album Quilt. Maddy had given up the idea of finishing hers, a traditional design known as Log Cabin Courthouse Steps.

Aggie had been working hard on her Crazy Quilt. Lizzie was coaching her, but careful to let the girl do it herself. That was the only way to learn.

~ ~ ~

While everybody was in a tizzy over the festival, Maddy decided to tidy up a few loose ends. The FBI might be satisfied that Mikhail Kuzmich was responsible for all the deaths, but she couldn't see a motive for poisoning Dr. K. Maybe N'yen was right about there being no connection between the two crimes.

If it were true about Veronica Kardashian playing around behind her husband's back, that put her name firmly at the top Maddy's suspect list. Hadn't Ephraim Wagler seen her *rutsching* with another doctor?

Did Veronica inject Dr. K with the polonium-210? No, that sounded more like the work her paramour. After all, a doctor would have more access to radioactive materials than a housewife might. And an injection – there had been a pinprick on Dr. K's forearm, according to the autopsy report – sounded more like the work of a doctor.

But who was this phantom physician?

Dr. Horace Prepper was a good candidate. Wasn't he the hospital's Chief Radiologist? He had access to radioactive isotopes; it would be easy for him to steal a tiny batch, wouldn't it?

But polonium-210? Where would the Radiology Department get polonium?

CHAPTER THIRTY-SEVEN

The Merry Widow

Somehow it seemed too pat to blame Dr. K's death on Russian spies. The Bone Man, yes. That plumber, yes. But Maddy just didn't see a connection between her vascular neurologist and a pack of Red spies.

Now feeling up to driving, she made a hair appointment at Helen of Troy Spa and Beauty Saloon. In booking her trim-and-touchup, she'd finagled Margie Yost into giving her an overlapping time with Veronica Kardashian. The *You're-Too-Vain* blonde had a regular date for every second Thursday, it turned out.

That's how Maddy found herself sitting in the next styling chair to the gay widow. Listening to her chatter to the beautician who was touching up her roots, you'd think the biggest tragedy in her recent life had been a losing hand at bridge last week.

"Excuse me for interrupting," said Maddy, "but I wanted to offer my condolences for your loss. I was one of your husband's patients."

"Oh yes, Maddy Madison. I remember Elmer mentioning that he was treating you. He said it was a mild stroke and you'd be back to normal quickly ... and here you are."

"Just trying to get back to human status after a week or two in the hospital."

"Yes, a trip to Helen of Troy will put you back on track."

"Will you be keeping in touch with any of your husband's colleagues? Or are other doctors too painful a reminder of your loss."

"I'm sure a few of them will remain in my social circle. Life goes on, as they say."

Maddy slipped in her zinger. "What about Dr. Prepper?"

"Who?"

"Horace Prepper, the hospital's Chief Radiologist."

"Oh, the one they call Pepper Upper. I don't know him very well. But Ralph Niedermayer, president of the hospital's board, has been a real dear. As has Dr. Blatt, Dr. Pettigrew, and Dr. Michaelson. I'm sure I'll be seeing them on the Burpyville social scene. They're all very outgoing people, as I'm sure you know."

Maddy had bumped into the Kardashians once at a party at Ralph Niedermayer's palatial estate. The Ridenours had dragged her and Beau along. Edgar was on the hospital board, a residual appointment from his banking days.

"Any other doctors on your social calendar?" probed Maddy. Hoping she wasn't going too far.

"No, not really. I was never really fond of the medical profession, with the exception of my husband and a few others. The friends I just mentioned."

"Well, I'm sure you need to go through your mourning period."

"No, not really," she repeated. "I don't believe in moping about. When you fall off the horse, get back on I always say. Don't you agree?"

Maddy blushed. "I'm not sure how I would handle it. I can hardly imagine life without Beau."

"As for me, I'm not done yet. I predict I will have found

me a new man by this time next year."

And a doctor to boot, thought Maddy.

~ ~ ~

Cookie was surprised to see a horse and buggy pull up in front of the Historical Society building. While Amish keep ties to the past, she'd never had one visit this repository of local history.

She knew of the Menno-Hof, a non-profit information center in Shipshewana that teaches about the Amish and Mennonites. A Swiss Heritage Society over in Berne, which concerned itself mainly with preservation of architectural landmarks. A Mennonite Historical Library located on the campus of Goshen College. And the Amish Acres in Nappanee that was the only Amish farm listed in the National Register of Historic Places. But the Old Order Amish kept largely to themselves, considering their history to be "a family matter." Family, meaning shared among the Amish themselves.

The figure who stepped out of the buggy surprised her: none other than Ephraim Wagler, every blued-eyed and square-chinned inch of him. He was a magnificent specimen of young manhood. Tall, sturdy, and handsome, his shaggy blond hair peeking from beneath a broad-brimmed straw hat.

She met him at the door. "Hello, Ephraim. Do come in."

"*Hoi, Frau* Bentley," he nodded politely. "I will stand out here if that suits you. *Ich mues öppis mälde.*"

"Yes – you have something to report?"

"As you know, we Amish practice non-resistance. We avoid conflict. We are private people who avoid contact with the outside world. It is better to not get to involved in affairs of the Englishers. Yet my mother says for me to tell you all."

"About what?"

"*Dä dokter.* The one who is *rutsching* with *Frau* Kardashian."

"Do you know his name?"

"*Nei*, but I can tell you this: he drives *es rosa auto onni es obertail.*"

"He drives what –?"

"*Es rosa auto* without a top."

"A pink convertible?"

"*Ja*, that is it."

"Thank you, Ephraim. You've been very helpful."

"He is a bad man?"

"Maybe. We need to find out."

"I must go now. I have work to do. The roof. Half done is far from done."

"Will you be joining us for Watermelon Days?"

"*Wassermelonä Daag*? *Nei*, it is best you Englishers celebrate your holidays with your own."

"All work and no play –?"

"There is much I must do. Soon I leave home to start my family. I have completed my 'running around' – *Rumspringa*, we call it. Me and Rachel Springer have been published. The wedding is to be next week."

"I thought most weddings take place in November."

"This is true. But Rachel is bound not to wait."

Cookie wondered if that meant an early baby was in the works. Bundling beds were not always an effective form of birth control. "My congratulations to you and Rachel."

"*Danke, Frau* Bentley. *Ich wünsch ihne e schöne Wassermelonä Daag.*"

"Think about coming. You and your family would be welcome."

CHAPTER THIRTY-EIGHT

Amish Quilts

*T*he Amish were slow at accepting change. So for a long time they used old German featherbeds and coverlets rather than piecing quilts like their neighbors. But gradually changes came. Very few Amish quilts were made before the 1870s; around then quilting became quite common.

Amish always used conservative styles, the earlier quilts made in one solid color – brown, blue, rust or black. Though the fabric was plain, the quilting done to hold the layers together was intricate and decorative. Swirling feathers, curves and grids were typical quilting patterns.

Fabric colors evolved to include deep and solid hues such as pumpkin, olive green and an occasional dark red.

As others moved on to elaborate Crazy Quilts, the Amish adopted the more basic of the block patterns. Nine Patch, Around the World, and Sunshine and Shadow were popular. Amish quilts were usually made of wool or cotton, silks considered too worldly.

During World War II natural fiber was hard to come by so even the Amish turned to the synthetics of that time. As most people turned away from quilting, considering it old-fashioned and a waste of time, the Amish continued the tradition. With the 1976 Bicentennial more Americans became interested in their past, and discovered the art of Amish quilting. Amish women began to produce quilts to be sold. Being busy in the garden in the milder months meant Amish quilting was mostly done in the winter.

The Amish still make quilts for their own use: weddings, babies, friendship and as fund-raisers. And Amish quilts continue to be a source of inspiration to quilters. Modern quilt artists are using black with solid colors and discovering the beauty in such basic designs.

~ ~ ~

Dan Sokolowski had given Lizzie Ridenour the info about a latter-day Amos Stoltzfus living north of Swisstown. No doubt about it, he had to be a relative of the long-lost Annabell's husband.

Curious, Lizzie drove up to Swisstown. She had already finished her quilt for Watermelon Days, and had nothing better to do. Besides, she felt she had to follow up on Annabell. After all, the young bride had reached out from beyond the grave to ask for her help. Not that there was anything that could be done at this late date.

Asking for directions at a Shell station led her to a log cabin near a curve in the Wabash River. Even though Stoltzfus had left the church, there was no car parked outside or electricity lines leading up to the house.

A tall white-haired man stepped onto the porch as Lizzie pulled up. "Hello," she shouted from her car window, "I'm looking for Amos Stoltzfus."

"That is me," he said. "Do I know you?"

"No, I live down in Caruthers Corners."

"What brings you to my door? I do not sell wooden tables anymore. My arthritis is too bad to do woodwork."

"Actually, I wanted to ask about an ancestor of yours, a man by the same name."

"Ay, I was named after *mi grospapi* ... grandfather, that is."

"What was your grandmother's name?" Lizzie asked as she stepped out of the car.

"Rebecca, why do you ask?"

"I thought his wife was named Annabell ... or Mary."

"*Nei, mi gromi* was Rebecca. But I am told he married before. The earlier wife could be Mary. That sounds right to my ear."

"How did the earlier wife die?"

"I know not. Old age, most likely."

"Was your grandfather wealthy."

"He was."

"How did he make his money?"

"Like me, he was a cabinetmaker."

"Are you rich?"

"*Nei*, I am not."

"Then how did he get rich?"

Amos Stoltzfus looked embarrassed. "There is family talk of a large dowry from the earlier wife ... Mary, you say her name is."

"What happened to the riches?" she pressed.

"He drank it away, *mi papi* told me. A family curse. I am known to take a sip of hard cider now and again myself."

"Are there any keepsakes from your grandfather's earlier wife?"

Stoltzfus shook his head. "We are not a sentimental family," he said.

Lizzie turned back to her car. "Thank you for your time," she said. "I must be going. It's a long drive back to Caruthers Corners."

"Wait!" he said. "Perhaps there is something."

Lizzie leaned against her car door as the man went into the house and returned carrying a small packet of envelopes.

"Here," he handed it to her. "These letters were in *mi papi*'s trunk. I do not know to who they belong. I do not read."

She untied the string and thumbed through the scant envelopes, three in all. Ahab Stoltzfus to a Sarah Yonzer. Ahab Stoltzfus to a Benjamin Stoltzfus. And *aha*! – Mary Stoltzfus to Whom It May Concern.

Unfolding the third letter, she read:

My husband is trying to kill me as he did his first wife Annabell. After Amos receives our dowry he has no further use for us. He will marry and kill again – which is why I am writing this letter to the future Mrs. Amos Stoltzfus. Amos cannot read so hopefully he will not decypher this message to you. He pretends to be an upstanding citizen, thus nobody will believe your claims. The only thing to do is kill him first. Tell him you have been seeing rats and he will buy rat poison. Stryknine, I think it is called. Feed him a large helping in his breakfast mash, the cornbread crumpled in milk he prefers. That should do the trick. I will leave this letter in his footlocker for you to find, expecting that you will be educated and capable of reading. You do not have to take my word for this: He will announce his intentions of killing you and laugh in your face. Therefore you must strike first. I did not act soon enough and fear I will be dead by his hands before the night is over.

(signed) Mrs. Mary Elizabeth Wagler Stoltzfus

Lizzie looked up at the old man. "How did your grandfather die?"

"Took stomach cramps. They say he died in agony, his wife at his bedside. He left her pretty well off, she and the child who would become my father."

"I'm told you were shunned. Do you mind saying why?"

"Simple. I married outside the church. Naomi is a good woman. We have been happy together for forty years."

~ ~ ~

Cookie was putting the finishing touches on her Amish Sunshine and Shadow quilt. She looked up when Lizzie appeared at her farmhouse door with the rest of the Quilters Club in tow. "What brings all of you out on this fine summer night?" she greeted them.

"We tried to call, but your cell phone goes to Voice Mail," Maddy explained.

"Oops, sorry."

"Lizzie brings news that couldn't wait. She has solved the murders of Annabell Yoder and Mary Wagler."

"Solved the murders –?"

"Yes, she discovered a letter that reveals all," nodded Bootsie. "A historic find, I think you'll agree."

Lizzie held up the slip of ruled writing paper. "A letter from beyond the grave," she said.

The women gathered around Cookie's kitchen table where the light was good and reread the letter from Mrs. Mary Elizabeth Wagler Stoltzfus. "This is like a murder confession," said the police chief's wife.

"Well, at least a confession of conspiracy in a crime committed by someone else," Cookie pointed out after Lizzie described how the original Amos Stoltzfus died.

177

"I'd call it justifiable homicide," Maddy opined.

"Ditto," said Bootsie.

"Double ditto," added Lizzie.

"I don't condone murder of any kind," muttered Cookie, rereading the letter. "But in this case I'd have to agree."

CHAPTER THIRTY-NINE

Watermelon Days

Mayor Mark Tidemore gave an inspiring speech, one that had constituents talking about him as the next candidate for governor. But that would never happen; Mark the Shark was much too liberal for a state like Indiana. Nonetheless Watermelon Days opened on an upbeat note this year.

Cookie Bentley acquitted herself well, too. Her talk about local history was followed by a reception in the new wing of the Caruthers Corner's Historical Society. The official opening was a huge success; 114 new members signed up.

The Watermelon Days Parade was spectacular – in its own small way. Practically all of the town's 3,012 population turned out, crowding Main Street and spilling over into the big town square. Even Abram and Abigail Wagler turned out with their fifteen kids, plus Ephraim's new wife Rachel and the entire Springer clan. Add to that 40- or 50,000 tourists.

Children ran through the crowds like wild Indians. Even a genuine Potawatomi named Metea Davis was on hand, operating a booth that sold "Red Injun Maize Pies" (which turned out to be cornbread smeared with butter and watermelon jam). Tilly's youngest, the ever-active Mandy, fell into the Jacob Caruthers Memory Pond near the bandstand, but fortunately it was only two-feet deep and the Tidemores lived in the big Victorian across the street, so dry clothing was readily available.

N'yen got to ride with the fire chief (his Uncle Freddie) in the shiny red fire engine; his job was to turn on the siren every block or so, not that there were very many blocks on Main Street.

Aggie fared even better. Dressed as an exotic princess, she got to ride atop Happy, the elephant from the town's petting zoo. Bombay Martinez had come out of retirement to lead Happy along behind the Caruthers High band.

Next came trucks pulling old circus cages (left over from when Haney Bros. was a traveling circus) that contained the lion and tiger and bear – oh my! And bringing up the rear was Sneezy the baboon. He waved at the crowd lining Main Street, apparently happy to be a celebrity again.

Clowns swarmed about the parade route, making faces at children and hugging pretty women and squirting seltzer water at each other. Bobby Ray Purdue – once known as Sprinkles the Clown – lead the organized coulrophobic riot. He'd bought clown costumes for the high school football team and trained them in the basics of buffoonery.

Monday's Watermelon Eating Contest brought no surprise. Fat Karl Schaeffer handily won. Then had room for desert, a watermelon pie.

However, Tuesday's Biggest Watermelon competition was an upset. While Boyd Aitkens brought in a watermelon even bigger that last year's winning entry, Sad Sammy Hankins bested him by two pounds. The judges measured the humongous watermelons twice, just to make sure – 316 pounds to 314. A sore loser, Boyd swore he'd get revenge in next years competition.

The big news was Lizzie Ridenour's win over former state champion Holly Eberhard in the Quilting Competition. Lizzie's Jacob's Ladder Quilt had been a *tour de force* of fine stitchery, the judges calling her design "clever, creative, and perfectly executed."

And even better news, Aggie's Crazy Quilt came in second in the Junior Competition. Not bad progress for a girl who'd never held a sewing needle until three years ago. Her Grammy threw a party for her and Lizzie.

N'yen had something to celebrate too. He won the Science Fair with his display on how to build a cyclotron. But no one was surprised by that, him being such a Brainiac. Even Major Gen. Calvin LaRosa stopped by the booth to congratulate him. And to check out the risk of the boy building an atomic bomb, Maddy guessed. The Air Force was still cleaning up the underground missile site at the end of Far Fields Road.

The party's unspoken purpose was to acknowledge Maddy's recovery from her stroke. She was back on her feet, functioning as normal, no residual effects. Dr. Blatt had pronounced her healthy ... and lucky.

~ ~ ~

On Wednesday night, everybody gathered at the Watermelon Days festivities. A carnival was going full blast on the town square, the highlight being the newly acquired Ferris wheel. The circular structure was festooned with twinkly lights, reds and yellows and blues. The slow-turning wheel was as hypnotic as a mesmerist's "vision spinner." Round and round and round.

Aggie and N'yen were hanging out with their friend Metea Davis at his "Red Injun Maize Pies" booth. Aggie got to butter; N'yen smeared on the jam. Metea did the cornbread baking in a small portable oven, something like a pottery kiln or pizza oven. Customers praised the homemade treat.

Tilly and Mark had joined Freddie and Amanda with their smaller children at the kiddie rides – a miniature choo-choo train and a six-horse merry-go-round. The kids squealed with delight as if they were riding wild broncos in the Old West.

The men folk – Beau, Jim, Ben, and Edgar – were smoking cigars over near the Town Hall, discussing the weather. It was a beautiful evening, with clear skies, 50% relative humidity, the temperature a perfect 74°. Rain a week away, according to the Channel 4 weathergirl.

Meanwhile, the women were gathered at the bandstand where Hoagie Henderson & His Hoosier All-Stars were playing "Ole Buttermilk Sky" (an Academy Award-nominee in 1946) and "In the Cool, Cool, Cool of the Evening" (winner of an Oscar for Best Original Song in 1951) – tributes to the bandleader's namesake, Hoagie Carmichael.

Born in Indiana, Hoagie Carmichael has been called "the most talented, inventive, sophisticated and jazz-oriented of all the great craftsmen of pop songs in the first half of the Twentieth Century." The Tin Pan Alley songwriter composed four of the most recorded songs of all time ("Stardust," "Georgia on My Mind," "The Nearness of You," and "Heart and Soul.") His music brought back memories.

Lurking nearby was a sinister figure, a tall man with heavy brows and a sharp chin, a hat pulled down to partially hide his face. He was eating a fried cheese ball, an attempt to blend with the crowd. Everybody seemed to be munching on something – corn dogs, sno-cones, fried tenderloins, cornbread with jam, DQ Blizzards – even fried cheese balls, a holdover from the local Swiss heritage.

He had spotted the four women standing near the bandstand, listening to those schmaltzy tunes.

> *"Lazybones, sleepin' in the shade*
> *How you 'spect to get your cornmeal made?*
> *You'll never get your cornmeal made*
> *Just sleepin in the evenin' shade ..."*

The question was whether to kill all four ... or simply take out their leader, the one known as "Maddy."

~ ~ ~

Maddy felt a tug on her arm. It was N'yen, impatiently trying to get her attention. "Grammy, take us on the Ferris wheel. Aggie and I want to see the town at night from up there on top of the wheel." At 65 feet, it was almost the tallest point in town, short of the spire atop Peaceful Meadows, the picturesque church on the far side of the town square.

"You're not tall enough," she clucked. "There's a height limit."

"Yes, I am. I grew over the summer. Come, let me show you."

The boy led her toward the lighted Ferris wheel. The device was turning like a wagon wheel, its gondolas packed with kids and teens. Next to the ticket booth was a sign that said YOU MUST BE THIS TALL TO RIDE.

N'yen fitted himself in front of the outstretched arm of

a wooden Bugs Bunny-like character to prove his new height, barely one inch to the good. "See, Grammy, I can ride."

"I've been tall enough for years," bragged Aggie, now in her early teens.

"I'm catching up," said N'yen. "I'll be taller than you by next year, just you wait and see."

"Good luck with that, shrimp," she teased.

"That's garlic ginger shrimp to you," he responded chipperly, citing his favorite stir-fry dish. A Vietnamese favorite.

"Here, let me buy us tickets," their grandmother said, fishing in her purse for her wallet. "Three, please," she said to the girl in the ticket booth.

"That's one dollar each. For charity."

"Excellent," Maddy beamed.

Almost ten o'clock, the crowds had thinned out. Caruthers Corners was an early-to-bed town. Maddy and the kids would be up next, the only people in line. The operator had paused the wheel, letting the gondolas rock back-and-forth up there in the nighttime sky, elucidating squeals from the excited riders.

Maddy stared up at the stopped wheel, wondering if she had the courage to climb aboard when their turn came. She'd always been slightly afraid of heights. But she'd promised the children.

"Hold on there, you meddling *dura*," came a harsh voice from behind her.

"Are you speaking to me?" Maddy turned toward the sound.

"Right you are, *suka*," replied the tall man holding a knife in one hand, a glass vial in the other.

Uh-oh. This didn't look good, Maddy told herself.

"*Popal. Prishju!*" A threat?

Was he speaking Russian? That would be her guess. Could this be the elusive Mikhail, the man who killed Hoppy Casals?

"Don't harm the children," she said, instinctively stepping away from them, more toward the Ferris wheel.

Mikhail Dmitriyevich Kuzmich followed her, swinging the knife blade in a smooth arc, slicing her across the forearm. Blood seeped out of the open cut, a garish red under the Ferris wheel lights.

"*Ti menia dostal, baba.*" He stepped closer to Maddy, raising the glass vial in the air. "*Zdohni!*"

Just then, N'yen reached for the lever that operated the Ferris wheel and yanked it forward. With a lurch, the wheel started to turn again, a gondola car swinging downward to crack Mikhail Kuzmich on the top of his skull. *Thunk!* The hat cushioned the blow, but it took him down nonetheless.

As the Russian fell, he dropped the vial. Maddy helplessly watched it tumble toward the cinder blocks that formed the boarding platform. But before it hit the cement, Aggie performed a perfect double tumble, catching the vial in mid-air. "Got it," she shouted, unaware of the poisonous U-235 concoction sloshing about inside the stoppered tube. She smiled proudly, having finally got the acrobatic move right.

"Better give me that," her grandmother said, carefully retrieving the glass vial. "Why don't you two go find your Uncle Jim? Tell him to hurry, before this jasper regains his senses."

"But your arm is bleeding," exclaimed Aggie.

"I'll be all right. After you find Uncle Jim, go get your Uncle Freddie. He's trained as a paramedic."

"Yes, Grammy," said N'yen, ready to go for help.

However, the Russian climbed to his feet, knife still in his hand. "Don't be so fast, *molokosos*," he growled, waving the blade at the boy. "*Zakolebal*. I will cut off your head. Then I will kill this *cuchka derganaya*," he nodded toward Maddy.

"*Potselui mou zhopy*," replied N'yen.

The Asian boy's use of Russian stopped Mikhail Kuzmich in his tracks, causing him to cock his head to one side as if he was questioning his ears. "Where did you learn that, *gnida*?"

"I read," said the boy.

"*Schas po ebalu poluchish, podonok!*" He stepped toward the boy, but out of the darkness came a blur, a blond man in dark clothing. *Smak!* – a fist landed on the Russian's jaw, downing him, the knife tumbling into the grass.

Mikhail Kuzmich was down for the count.

"Ephraim, thank you!" Maddy said to the young man who had saved them from the Russian.

Ephraim Wagler ducked his head. "I-I have disobeyed the *Ordnung*," he stammered. "Our rules ask that we live as pacifists and strongly reject all physical violence. I have strayed from the Church and must face shunning by my family."

"But you saved our lives," countered Cookie from the

sidelines.

"Yes," nodded Bootsie. "You're a hero."

"And a handsome one," added Lizzie.

"But Matthew 5:38-42 tells us, '*You have heard that it was said, "An eye for an eye, and a tooth for a tooth." But I tell you, do not resist an evil person. If someone strikes you on the right cheek turn to him the other also. And if someone wants to sue you and take your tunic, let him have your cloak as well. If someone forces you to go one mile, go with him two miles. Give to the one who asks you, and do not turn away from the one who wants to borrow from you.*'"

"Son," boomed a voice from the darkness. "I saw what occurred." Abram Wagler stepped forward. "No, you shall not be shunned. Palms 97:10 tells us, "*You who love the Lord, hate evil! He preserves the souls of His saints; He delivers them out of the hands of the wicked.*' You are merely acting as the arm of God, delivering these good people from the wicked. That is permissible in this circumstance, I am certain."

"*Merci merci vielmal dangge,*" said the young man. "I want to start off my new married life without blemish." He held out his arm for his wife Rachel to come join him.

The bonneted young woman rushed to his side. "You were so brave," she whispered, almost afraid to say the words out loud.

"*Jetz isch färtig lusch!*" said his father. "Time it is to go home. Come everybody." The more-than-a-dozen Amish – ranging in age from four-years-old to sixty – clustered around Abram Wagler. "This is enough excitement with the Englishers for one night."

CHAPTER FORTY

The Real Killer

"That's him, that's Mikhail Kuzmich," nodded Bootsie, remembering his face from the Wal-Mart personnel files.

The man on the ground shook his head, as if trying to silence the ringing bells. *"Past' zabej, padla jebanaja,"* he said to the police chief's wife.

Chief Jim Purdue snapped the cuffs on his prisoner. "Put a cork in it," he growled. "You're under arrest for murder, attempted murder, and spitting on the sidewalk."

"Oyobuk."

"Petie," he said to his deputy, "put him in the lock-up. I'll call the FBI. This is the guy Neil Wannamaker's been looking for – a genuine Russian spy. He's the guy that killed Dr. K, the Bone Man, and Hoppy Casals."

"No," said Maddy. "He didn't kill Dr. Kardashian."

"What?" Jim Purdue practically swallowed his tongue.

"Dr. Kardashian was a separate murder with a separate motive. But there is a connection, which is why that Bone Man – Willard G. Manchester, or Viktor Ivanovich Medvedev to use his real name – was executed by Mikhail."

"If Mikhail Kuzmich didn't murder Elmer Kardashian, who did?"

Maddy spotted Veronica Kardashian in the gathering crowd of onlookers. "Her lover," she pointed at the blonde.

"I beg your pardon!" exclaimed the widow. "My what?"

"The doctor you've been seeing on the side."

"And who would that be?" she snorted.

"The one with the pink convertible."

"Dr. Pettigrew, you're saying?"

So that's who owned the pink car. "Yes, the head of the Toxicology Department at Burpyville Memorial."

"You're accusing Dr. Felix Pettigrew of murder?" blurted Lizzie's husband who had joined the others under the Ferris wheel. Serving on the hospital board, Edgar Ridenour knew most of the doctors.

"Yes, ol' Felix's quite the womanizer." She remembered him with the cute Candy Striper. "Little surprise he was attracted to a sophisticated lady like Veronica Kardashian."

"Really!" the blonde said. "You have quite a nerve, Mrs. Madison." She turned to walk away.

"Don't go yet," called Maddy. "I'm about to reveal how Dr. Pettigrew did it."

Veronica Kardashian whirled around to face her accuser. "Everybody knows Elmer was poisoned with polonium, a poison only used by the Russians." She nodded toward Mikhail Kuzmich, who was now sitting up, rubbing his jaw. That Amish fellow had packed quite a punch.

"No, your husband was actually poisoned with uranium-235, a radioactive material retrieved from a Titan-II missile by Hoppy Casals."

"But Casals was working for the Russians."

"How did you know that, if not from someone involved in your husband's death?"

"Well, uh, I –"

"Dr. Pettigrew gave a false toxicology report in order to cast suspicion on the Russians. But he used good ol' USA uranium to commit the murder."

"But you just said that Casals fellow stole the uranium from that missile for the Russians."

"No, you said it was for the Russians. And you're correct in that. Mikhail Kuzmich and Viktor Medvedev paid Hoppy Casals $50,000 to steal the U-235 from a nuclear warhead in our own backyard. A missile silo out on Far Fields Road."

There was a gasp from the crowd.

"Dr. Pettigrew approached an intern in the Radiology Department to buy some sort of radioactive isotope, little realizing the man was a Russian spy – what they call an Agent in Place. Eager to make some quick money on the side, the ersatz Willard G. Manchester sold him a few milligrams of the stolen U-235. And when the Russian masterminds found out about Medvedev's little side deal, they ordered Kuzmich to execute him. A bullet to the back of the head."

"Why do that?" asked Chief Purdue.

"To cut off any traces between them and Dr. Kardashian's murder. They were hoping no one would learn of their uranium heist. After all, hardly anyone remembered that underground missile silo after all these years."

"But Hoppy Casals became a threat," Bootsie added. "So they had Mikhail Kuzmich get rid of him too with a little taste of the U-235."

"If the Russians were getting rid of all loose ends, how come Dr. Pettigrew is still running around unscathed," sniffed Veronica Kardashian, as if that blew Maddy's theory.

"Where is Dr. Pettigrew?" asked Maddy. "Didn't he bring you to the festival tonight?"

"That doesn't prove anything," the blonde huffed.

"Pettigrew was right here a minute ago," said Ben Bentley. "He left when you started pointing the finger at him and Mrs. K."

"Look," someone said. "There's a pink convertible parked over near the Town Hall. Didn't you say that's what he drives?"

"Yeah, a flashy pink Caddy," another bystander confirmed.

Everyone looked toward the car parked in front of the Town Hall. Just then the Caddy's headlights flipped on and the engine roared – followed immediately by a gigantic explosion.

Ka-Boom!

The convertible went up in flames. A bomb hooked to the ignition.

Maddy turned back to Mikhail Kuzmich. "Well, well, you've been a busy boy tonight – trying to kill me and succeeding in murdering Dr. Pettigrew."

Kuzmich sneered. "*Po'shyol 'na hui.*"

Maddy shrugged. "I'm not sure what you said, but I'm positive it's rude."

"He said –" N'yen began.

"Never mind," his grandmother hushed him. "No need to repeat such rubbish."

"You can't prove any of this," sniffed Veronica Kardashian. "It's all lies." Obviously no more perturbed over Dr. Pettigrew's death than she was over the demise of her husband.

"If there's no truth in this, you can hold this vial," Maddy thrust the glass tube in the blonde's direction. "The solution inside probably isn't radioactive at all."

"*Egad!*" she squealed, backing away. "Get that uranium away from me."

"That was meant for this busybody woman. Pour it onto that cut and she be – how you say? – a goner."

Veronica Kardashian had regained her composure. "There's your guilty party," she nodded toward the Russian. "Since you can't prove my involvement in any of this, I'm going home if I can find a ride."

"As a matter of fact, we can prove your guilt," Aggie spoke up.

Veronica Kardashian gave the girl a withering smile. "Really, my dear. Exactly how would a cute little thing like you do that?"

"Simply by asking him," she pointed toward a figure running toward the flaming car.

Mrs. Kardashian followed the girl's gaze. "Why that's Felix. He wasn't in the car after all."

"Then who was?" said Maddy.

"I'd guess Johnny Bristol," sighed Police Chief Jim Purdue.

EPILOGUE

Yep, Dr. Felix Pettigrew spilled the beans. Veronica had urged him to get rid of her husband. There was a large insurance policy, it turned out. Not surprisingly, she was more interested in the money than in *rutsching* with the horny toxicologist.

He admitted it had been his plan to bribe an intern to filch some radioactive isotopes from the Radiology Department. The idea being once the underling learned of his role in a murder, he wouldn't dare blow the whistle.

Dr. Pettigrew figured he could deflect suspicion away from himself or the hospital's Radiology Department with a false toxicology report that pointed to a radioactive element that neither he nor the hospital would have access to – the elusive polonium-210.

What are the chances real Russian spies would get in the way of his plan?

By selling him stolen uranium, the lowly intern had gotten himself killed. And that brought on a reprisal against that plumber who'd assisted the Russians in stealing the uranium from an abandoned Titan missile ... as well as the attempt on Dr. Pettigrew's life with a firebomb. Dang, he'd loved that pink convertible. It had been a real chick magnet.

The Nuclear Regulatory Commission had helped bury the story. Forgotten ICBMs were not good publicity. The *Burpyville Gazette* didn't mention where the Russians had gotten their radioactive poison. You'd think they bought it across the counter at CVS.

Dr. Pettigrew and Veronica were enjoying extended vacations courtesy of the Federal government. And once they finished serving sentences for illegal possession of U-235, they had murder charges to face.

Mikhail Dmitriyevich Kuzmich was locked away on a variety of espionage charges. The murder trial might never take place. Word was, Mikhail would return to Mother Russia in a quiet prisoner exchange. Well trained, Mikhail never identified his controller or said what happened to the missing uranium. Returning home was his reward.

Perhaps Annabell and Mary finally found peace, with the revelation that Rebecca avenged them and saved herself.

Aggie passed gymnastics and preserved her honor role status. N'yen returned to his family in Chicago, displaying his Science Fair award to all he encountered.

And Maddy? To her pleasant surprise, a write-in vote elected her as this year's Watermelon Days Queen.

Thank you for reading. Please review this book. Reviews help others find Absolutely Amazing eBooks and inspire us to keep providing these marvelous tales. If you would like to be put on our email list to receive updates on new releases, contests, and promotions, please go to AbsolutelyAmazingEbooks.com and sign up.

Bonus

By going to the Absolutely Amazing eBooks online website (AbsolutelyAmazingEbooks.com) and entering the password below into the Bonus Reward Section, you can access recipes for many of the dishes you read about in this book – for free!

AA1056

About the Author

Marjory Sorrell Rockwell says needlecraft arts – quilting, crocheting, knitting – are pastimes every woman can appreciate. And she particularly loves quiltmaking. "It's like painting with cloth," she says. But when not quilting she writes mysteries about a Midwestern sleuth not unlike herself, a middle-aged lady with an unpredictable family and loyal friends. And she's a big fan of watermelon pie.

ABSOLUTELY AMA⚡ING eBOOKS

AbsolutelyAmazingEbooks.com
or AA-eBooks.com